The Lemon Grove

For Marsha
With best wishes
Ali Hosseini

5.12.14
Rockland

ALI HOSSEINI

The Lemon Grove

CURBSTONE BOOKS

NORTHWESTERN UNIVERSITY PRESS

EVANSTON, ILLINOIS

Curbstone Books
Northwestern University Press
www.nupress.northwestern.edu

Printed in the United States of America

10   9   8   7   6   5   4   3   2   1

This is a work of fiction. Characters, places, and events are the product of the author's imagination or are used fictitiously and do not represent actual people, places, or events.

The book's epigraph is reprinted from *The Collected Poems of Weldon Kees,* edited by Donald Justice, by permission of the University of Nebraska Press. Copyright 1962, 1975, by the University of Nebraska Press. Copyright © renewed 2003 by University of Nebraska Press.

Library of Congress Cataloging-in-Publication Data
Hosseini, Ali.
    The lemon grove / Ali Hosseini.
        p. cm.
    ISBN 978-0-8101-2829-3 (pbk. : alk. paper)
    I. Title.
    PS3608.O823L46 2012
    813.92—dc23

                                                                        2012002151

∞ The paper used in this publication meets the minimum requirements of the American National Standard for Information Sciences—Permanence of Paper for Printed Library Materials, ANSI Z39.48-1992.

To my mother

and brothers

and sisters

and the memory

of my father

Burn, glare, old sun, so long unseen,
That time may find its sound again, and cleanse
What ever it is that a wound remembers
After the healing ends.

—WELDON KEES

The Lemon Grove

One

T HE DOOR FLIES OPEN and the room floods with sharp sunlight. Through half-closed eyes, I see someone standing, stick
in hand, surrounded by a halo of light and dust.

"Ah, you've recovered. Finally."

It's an old man's voice, a raspy voice that gives away his age. He
steps closer and stands above me. I realize I'm lying flat on the dirt
floor. My mouth is dry and my breathing heavy. He bends over and
stares at my face with one eye. His other eye is a black hole that appears and disappears as he blinks.

Above me a small shaft of sunlight falls into the room from the
broken ceiling. I twist my neck around and recognize the old plaster
walls and broken window. I'm at the farmhouse. Outside are the
trees of the Naranjestan, the old lemon grove. But who is this man?
I wonder if he is an informer.

I reach out and try to get up, but the wall runs away from me
and the ground becomes a cradle under my feet. I seem to lack any
natural connection to the earth and suddenly lose control and fall
forward on my chest.

"What are you doing?" he says, helping me to turn over on my back. "Take it easy."

He brings his hand to my forehead. His skin is cold against my face.

"You're burning with fever. But thank God you're alive. It's a miracle. With all the poison you've drunk, I thought for sure we would lose you."

Who is he? Has he followed me here?

"Leave me alone," I murmur. I try to get up again, but my face is not even an inch from the ground when my head goes into a spin. I feel like I'm going to be sick, but there is nothing left inside me. I have to get up. I have to run away but have no energy left. I shut my eyes and give in to exhaustion.

"What were you trying to prove, young man?" he says. "Did you have a contest with the death angel?" He steps back. "I must say, I got here just in time. What were you thinking? The life that God has granted us, only he should take away—and when he desires. Taking your life or someone else's is not in your or my hands."

He spreads an old kilim beside the wall and takes my hand.

"Can you make it over here?" he asks in a kind voice.

I look at him standing above me.

"Come on," he says. "It's not good to be on the bare floor. Come lie down here. You must rest now. You need energy to recover."

I search for my hands, my legs, my head. I feel them, but it's as if they were scattered all around me. I can't concentrate and my thoughts are dispersed—here, there, nowhere. I slowly stretch out my legs, feeling that if I get up, all my bones will crumple into a blind knot. My insides turn and twitch with every little move.

He pulls me onto the faded kilim and sits down by the door with his legs crossed and his back to the wall. He takes off his old frayed cap and places it on his knee. His face is sunburned and there are lines of dried salt on his neck. He smells of milk and wool. Who is this man and what is he doing here? My tiredness and numbness do not give way to clear thoughts.

He opens a sack in front of him. "I've brought you some *nan-o-kabab*—bread and *kabab*—and a jar of water. *Kabab* is good for a poisoned stomach. You have to eat—you need to get some energy."

His voice is familiar. Have I heard it not long ago?

"When I found you, you were half-dead. I fed you milk. That's the reason you're alive. I milked a few of my sheep. You're lucky—only a couple of them have milk at this time of year."

He looks out through the half-open door then turns to me.

"Do you remember anything about what happened?"

I stay silent.

"I understand. You don't want to talk. You're exhausted. I had to open your mouth and pour the milk in. Then I kept bending your legs onto your chest until you threw it all up, the poison and the milk. I had to do it four or five times, until your stomach was empty."

I close my eyes and try to remember, but nothing comes to mind. I wish that he would go away so I could die alone. He glances at me for a moment, then turns and looks out through the cracked door. He seems to be waiting for someone. Are there others who know I'm here? Have the men who took Shireen away now found me too?

He picks up a piece of *nan,* wraps it around a chunk of *kabab,* and hands it to me. The wrinkled skin around his blind eye quivers.

"Here," he says. "Eat."

The smell of the *kabab* brings a bitter taste to my mouth.

"You must eat. If your stomach stays empty, you'll get an ulcer."

I push his hand away. I'm thirsty and my mouth is so dry I can hardly move my tongue. I wish he would give me some water.

"Well, young man, I know who you are, and I'm shocked by what you tried to do. I come here every day about noon to get away from the burning sun and the wind. I bring my animals and draw water from the well. They rest in the shade of the trees and I take a nap. Yesterday I saw that the door was open and you were lying inside. At first I thought you were asleep. Then I saw foam coming out of your mouth. I could see only the whites of your eyes. A pesticide bottle was next to you. You had thrashed around all over the floor and were covered with dirt."

I look at my fingers. My nails are broken and edged with dried blood. I become aware that they are smarting.

"I didn't know what to think. 'Oh, no—Ruzbeh!' I said, 'You finally did it. You finally got tired of wandering in the desert and committed the forbidden act.' Then I held up your head and looked at your face. 'He looks like Ruzbeh,' I thought, 'but where is the scar on his forehead?' That was when I realized it was you, Behruz. The only way I can tell you two apart is by the mortar-shell scar on your brother's forehead. I've seen you only a couple of times since you came back from America. Once was when you brought your mother and Ruzbeh from Shiraz to stay in the village. And then when you came here in a Jeep with Shireen, looking for Ruzbeh after he ran away. Both times I wanted to talk to you about the Naranjestan and what I was afraid was going to happen to it, but you were in such a hurry that I thought you wouldn't be interested in hearing what I had to say."

He pauses, as if waiting for me to reply, then continues.

"I've visited your mother a few times since she came to live in the village. She told me she had to leave the city because Ruzbeh was terrified by the sound of the Iraqi bombers and she was afraid as well. She brought him to the village, but still he ran away. I told her I would look for him. May God be with him wherever he is. I know you avoided this place after you came back from America. You saw it in ruin and left it to deteriorate further, but look how you've come back here now. It was God's will, of course. His plan was that I would save you. I believe he wanted you to live."

I look at him as he goes on talking but can't concentrate. I look at him, trying to see if I can recognize him. Wrinkles curve around his blind eye and join the deeper lines on his forehead. With an old handkerchief he wipes the sweat from his face, a face so full of lines it's as if he had lived life fourfold.

"Probably you don't know me," he says after a moment. "But you might, I'm not sure. If you remember your childhood when you used to come here from the city, you should remember me as well. I'm Musa—Musa Solimani."

In the far part of my memory I can see him, driving his herds to the farm on an early summer morning, helping Haji Zaman around the pump house, and making a fire for Father's water pipe and bringing it to him with a pot of tea on a tray. But he was younger then and not bent over. And his eye?—it was not like this.

"This place has been good to me. I used to work for your father,

God rest his soul, and then later I would work for your brother, Ruzbeh, before he was injured in the war. I helped with accounting and hiring the workers at harvesttime. Your parents were always kind to my family—they were kind to everyone, to the villagers too. But people these days are so selfish and lack any loyalty or sincerity."

I start to cough and my throat burns. I shut my eyes and try to block out his voice.

"I know you're not feeling well, but if you eat, you'll feel better. You'll be all right in a week or two."

He stares at me, expecting me to say something. His face is twitching as if he's in pain. Then he holds out the *nan* and *kabab* to me. I push his hand away again.

"Well, it looks like you're going to survive and when you're well, we'll try to find Ruzbeh. I'm sure you can help him to get well and both of you can make this place come to life again. It would make your mother very happy. I'm sorry, but I've got to tell you a few things. It's important and there isn't much time. Some of the villagers are planning to take over this land, this parched Naranjestan. After Ruzbeh disappeared into the desert, I came to the city to tell you, but you weren't anywhere to be found. I went to your mother, in the village. I told her. But she had lost all hope after Ruzbeh went away."

I think for a moment that I should go see Mother. But then, she probably doesn't want to see me. She would rather see Ruzbeh. It's he who is her "little one," born only minutes after me. She probably blames me for his running away, and seeing me would only make her miss him more.

Maybe she's right to blame me. I've been disillusioned with everything since I came back from America—with the outcome of the revolution and with my friends who supported all this madness so blindly. What else was there except to sink into daydreams of America? I wonder if Mother knows about what happened to Shireen. She must, with all the talking that people do around here, with all the spying that goes on.

He offers me the food again.

"You must eat. Just a little and we'll see if your stomach accepts it. Eat so you won't lose the dear life you've gained once more. It's God's will that you stay alive. He watches over all of us. Good or bad, He does. It's our own doing that puts us in odd situations. You're an educated man. You're young and more capable than people around here. Like your father, God rest his soul."

He looks toward me for some type of acknowledgment.

"You've been to America. You've traveled to the other side of the earth. I know that life isn't easy here, but that doesn't mean we should give up."

I feel hot and cold at the same time and a moment later am drenched with sweat. I hear his words but can't focus as sounds and images overcome me.

. . . There is a swarm of people in the square shouting that I'm the sinner, the heretic who returned from America to do a shameful act and should die. They say I harmed my brother, who had been injured in the war . . .

I try to see out through the cracked door and listen for any sound. If they come, if they find me here, how could I run? And where could I run to? I should go and hide in the desert. A long death under the blazing sun would be far easier than being dragged into the city square to meet the mad chanting and the flying stones.

The old man keeps talking like he's not had a companion all his life.

"Here," he says, holding the *kabab* closer. "Eat a little so you can survive. I'll give you some water later. It's not good to drink on an empty and bruised stomach."

Without thinking, I take the food from his hand. For a moment I stare at the cold *kabab* but can't bring myself to take a bite.

He is quiet for a moment and then, as if remembering something, goes on. "Well, anyway. You've been saved. Saved by milk. Milk is the source of life. From the moment that we come out of our mothers' wombs, we scream for it. If there were no milk, we would die. Our mothers' milk keeps us alive, cleans our insides from any poisons that we might be born with. Did you know if it happens that a lamb eats some poisonous greens, it must be fed milk to wash its stomach out? I've saved many lambs that way. Just like I did with you. Why do you keep looking at me? Eat. Eat so you stay alive."

I try to bite into the *kabab*. My mouth is so dry and numb that I taste nothing. My jaw hurts. The food falls from my hand. The old man, agitated, leans closer, pushing me with his hand.

"Why did you drop it?"

I look at him. His eye is blinking rapidly.

"Don't just stare at me. I said, why did you drop it? Pick it up and eat it. Would you like me to feed it to you the way I fed you the milk?"

I keep silent.

"Can't you say something? I'm trying to talk to you."

He turns and looks outside again. I hope he is thinking he should get up and leave. He moves closer to me.

"Here, drink a little water. I know you're thirsty, but it would be better if you eat first. Drink just a little, and then you must eat some food."

He hands me the jar. I drink hurriedly, water running down my neck.

"Easy, easy. That's enough." He takes the jar from me. "We'll see how your stomach reacts, and then we'll give you a little more."

He passes me a piece of food. Mechanically I obey and put it in my mouth.

"Good. Eat slowly. Good."

The food scratches my throat as it goes down. I can eat only a few small pieces and drop the rest on the floor.

"Okay. It's enough for now. Lie down and rest."

I stretch out and close my eyes. A moment later I feel feverish.

. . . The angry voices return along with the chants of a prayer. Groups of women covered in black chadors are gathered in the square. There is a noise, a creaking noise . . .

I open my eyes. The old wooden door is swinging back and forth in a continuous movement and I don't see Musa anywhere.

Two

I'M AWAKE BUT AM HAVING TROUBLE keeping my eyes open. It must be morning. I look around and am able to make out some of the things in the room. There are empty cans of motor oil scattered around. A few old shovels with chipped edges are propped in a corner, and beside one of the walls is a pile of ashes and brush.

I can't say how long I've been lying here. The old man must have put the pillow under my head and spread the blanket over me. I push the blanket off and notice that my shirt is torn and its buttons gone. I sit up and see a water jar and a tied-up sack that the old man must have left.

When did I get here? Was it yesterday or the day before that I ran away from the city? The shouts of "Allah-o Akbar, Allah-o Akbar"—God is Great, God is Great—echoed in my head on the slow bus ride over the mountains to the village road. Darkness was descending when, running and walking, I reached the Naranjestan. The thirsty Naranjestan with the old lemon trees and crumbling farmhouse has fallen into disrepair since Ruzbeh hasn't been able to attend to it.

I came to find you, Ruzbeh. To find you and tell you what happened to Shireen and what happened in the square. But you're not here. And you weren't here a month ago when I rushed back after they took Shireen away, when everything changed for us. I wanted to ask your forgiveness but couldn't find you. Even with all my fear, I returned to the city, thinking maybe you had gone back home. I waited until nightfall before going to the house, but the militia in their green uniforms were in the yard waiting for me. They were waiting to drag me away like they had Shireen. I had to hide in the parks and under bridges for almost a month, searching for you and waiting to hear some news about Shireen.

After what I saw in the square a few days ago—was it really only a few days ago?—I came here again. I ran not from the zealots and the militia who were looking for me but from myself. I crouched here in the corner, enraged at myself and you, who were nowhere to be found. I escaped from their anger only to hear their shouts all around me in the darkness. Was I going out of my mind? I held my head in my hands trying to free myself from all the pain. Then in the dim moonlight creeping in from the broken ceiling, I saw the bottles in the corner of the room.

The dust-covered bottles were there in a row just where they had always been. A strange feeling awakened within me that took me back to the old days, our childhood days when we always wanted to open one of the bottles. We'd been warned by Father not to ever touch them, but we were fascinated. The secrets inside the bottles intrigued us. The demons and jinnis that were inside called to us to open the bottles so they could jump out and, in return for their freedom, grant our childish wishes as in the stories Father read to us from *One Thousand and One Nights*. We liked the good jinnis and wished they would appear to us. We hated the bad ones, who, according to the old stories, stole children or exchanged their babies for human children, because, so the legend goes, they liked human babies. Mother also forbade us to go to the pesticide room, saying that if we touched the bottles, even with the tip of a finger, we would drop dead right there, like the butterflies that covered the ground after the Naranjestan was fumigated.

I opened one of the dust-covered bottles. It hissed and a dark liquid oozed out, running down the sides and dripping on the ground. I moved quickly, as if I had desired the moment for a long time. Fire poured down my throat, but I kept drinking. Suddenly I started to cough, my body twisting, my chest collapsing. Then I felt calm and light, as if I were floating. Blackness slowly gathered, engulfing me. I didn't close my eyes and could see stars sparkling everywhere around, but the air became heavy and I remember I was hot and sweaty, then cold and shivering. I wanted to get up, but the ground gave way beneath me. I went down and down, circling and swirling so fast I couldn't keep my eyes open.

I don't know how long I lay there unconscious before I heard a voice, as if in the distance, ordering me to open my mouth, and then I didn't remember anything until the old man said he came along and saved me. He saved me from dying and here I am with the memory of the horrifying event at the city square that will continue to haunt me. There is no salvation from that. I wonder where the old man is now. From the door I can see the trees of the lemon grove bending in the wind, the same trees that shaded us from the sun when we used to run underneath them.

In the happier times, we used to come here from Shiraz in the old VW that Father loved to drive—Mother in front and us in the back, delighted that there was no more schoolwork and we were going to stay in the Naranjestan. From the farmhouse we could look out toward the village, shimmering in the bright summer sun. Then we would see two dark shadows on the road, a small one beside a tall one, and know that it was Shireen and her mother, Bibi Khanom, come to help Mother with the cooking and cleaning. We waited for Shireen. Her black hair was always in braids on the sides of her face, and her light-green eyes, unusual for an Iranian, mesmerized us.

There were many insects in the Naranjestan flying or jumping around and many butterflies going from blossom to blossom as we ran and tried to catch them. Father would sit in the shade of the willow beside the channel that carried the water from the pump house to the wheat fields. He would drink his tea, smoke his water pipe, and give orders to Haji Zaman, Shireen's stepfather.

We would often go and watch Haji Zaman while he operated the equipment in the pump house and told the field-workers what to do. He was called Haji even though he hadn't traveled to Mecca to fulfill the Islamic pilgrimage. We watched his limping figure as he moved around in a hurry and tried to stay away from his tense gaze and angry shouting. And when Ruzbeh imitated his limping walk, I laughed and encouraged him to do it more.

In the spring, Haji Zaman would empty the pesticide bottles into a huge plastic bucket of water and stir it with a stick. Then he would help the Afghani workers fill the spraying pumps and strap them to their backs. The Afghans had bushy mustaches and would look at us with sad eyes. We were afraid they were going to steal us, put us in sacks on their backs, and take us to Afghanistan. They were probably just missing the children they had left behind.

We watched while they sprayed the Naranjestan, listening to the hissing of the pumps and watching the soft clouds cover the leaves and blossoms. Later we would walk through the Naranjestan and pick up the butterflies that had fallen to the ground and were trying to take to the air. We would put them in the sun and watch them for hours, hoping they would recover and fly away. In those years the Naranjestan was sick and no one ever figured out exactly what kind of disease it was.

Ruzbeh, where are you now? I wish you would come so we can talk the way we used to those summer nights. So we could watch the stars again. So we could look for the Big Dipper, like we used to. The stars seemed so close we would try to touch them. I couldn't, but you said you did. You said if I stood on my toes and stretched up my arms, I could touch a star. I tried many nights but could never reach them, could never touch anything in the darkness above me. You said, "Think of your favorite girl and try to catch her star." You would stand up and raise your hand, twirling it in the dark and then bringing down your closed fist, saying, "See, I caught one." When you opened your hand I almost thought I could see a shining spot in your palm.

How we loved it here when the Naranjestan was green, when the pump with its *top, top, top* sound sent the water to the trees and the fields. The orchard was alive then, and the nearby desert felt far away. How you loved the nights—the silence of the fields and the stars. And how we loved Shireen. Later, after high school, it was love that kept you here. You stayed, and we both knew why. We knew that Shireen loved both of us and would have to chose between us. So one had to go and one had to stay. I decided to be the one to go. And you understood, just as I would have if you had been the one to leave. It was love that made me go to America—love for you and Shireen.

Besides, you always had the support of Mother, who couldn't stand your being away from her. You were her small boy. You were born not more than ten breaths after me but you were her "little one." She couldn't have borne the idea of your leaving for a foreign land. So it was I who went away. We had never been separated until then. Even in school, we had always been in the same class. For six long years I missed you—and missed Shireen. I went away, thinking it would make things easier for all of us. For you and Shireen, so you could be together without any shadow over your lives. For Mother too, who never quite trusted me and always worried I was a bad influence. I knew she could part with me but that it was out of the question to send both of us away.

Three

A HAND IS SHAKING ME. "Wake up, Behruz. Wake up."
I open my eyes and see Musa standing above me. He takes
my hand and helps me sit up.

"I let you sleep all afternoon while I went to check on my herds.
I need to take them back to the village soon. I've made some tea.
Here, have a cup. It will be good for your stomach. I'll come back
and bring you something to eat."

He sits by the door, then takes off his hat and rubs his fingers over
his short hair. "I'm glad that in the two days you've shown so much
progress. I believe the danger is over."

I drink the tea slowly, its warmth soft inside me. The sleep has
done me some good. I feel more rested and am breathing easier.

"Whatever God wants will be," he says, wiping his face with a
handkerchief.

"Let me tell you a story so you can understand what I'm talking
about." He looks out toward the fields, cocking his head. "It's been
said that in the olden times there was a king who wished for a son.
Finally God granted him a beautiful boy. A son so handsome that

people were proud of having such a prince and would come from all over the kingdom just to have a glimpse of him. The king, afraid that something might happen to his son, asked his astronomers to look into the heavens and find out how the prince would meet his death. The astronomers went to their books and looked into the sky for seven days and seven nights. Finally they told the king that the death of the prince would be caused by a scorpion. Hearing that, the king became silent for three days. Then he spoke. He ordered a glass palace to be built and put the prince inside. One day when the prince was seven years old, he asked his nanny why he wasn't allowed to go out into the garden and had to watch everything from behind glass walls. The nanny told him the finding of the astronomers—Now see the power of the Almighty—Hearing the reason, the prince wanted to see what a scorpion looked like. The nanny thought a bit and then made a small scorpion out of clay and put it in the prince's palm. As soon as the clay scorpion touched the prince's flesh, it came alive and stung him. You see? How can we know what plan God has for us? You come to this desert, to a place where you think there is no one around, but suddenly someone comes from nowhere and saves you. Yes. One who wants to live dies in a mysterious way and one who wants to die is saved in a mysterious way."

He pours me another cup of tea.

"Where was I?" he says after a moment. "Ah, yes. I've heard that the ruins of the glass palace are somewhere in the desert not far from here. I've spent all my life in this arid land. I know every up and down of it, from here to the far side of the plain and the mountains beyond. But I haven't seen the ruins of any palace. No . . . But there is a place beside one of those little hills . . ." He points outside the door. "Every time I go there I hear a whisper, like sand sliding over glass. Maybe there is something there, under those hills."

Then as if remembering something, he starts to search the pockets of his old coat, going from one to the other. Finally he finds what he was looking for and hands it to me.

"When I found you, you were holding this."

I take the key. It's Shireen's key to the courtyard of our house in Shiraz. My heart jumps and I feel sick at the sight of it . . . the voices come alive in my head, loud and demanding, when they stopped Shireen from turning the key to come in and started interrogating her, wanting to know who she was, who she was there to see. And I was shivering on the other side of the door, not having the courage to unlock it.

I open my fist and stare at the key. It's the last thing that carried her touch. I found it the night they took her away and always kept it with me. Maybe if I could tell someone, perhaps this old man, the voices and images would finally go away. But how can I put it into words?

Forgive me, Shireen—forgive me. Fear kept me from opening the door. Fear kept me rooted. Later I went back searching for you, hoping they'd let you go. I was terrified walking down the alley. Terrified that the militia, and among them the zealots, were waiting at the house to grab me. I knew that in their eyes and by their laws we had committed a sin. A sin that required the worst kind of punishment—not in the afterlife, but in this life, a punishment from the horrible depths of religion's history.

I was afraid to go into our house so I turned around and walked back into the street. Our Jeep wasn't there. They must have taken it along with everything inside the house. In the dim light of the alley I saw the key. It was on the ground next to the door. I knew you had dropped it when they took you away.

You were late coming back home from your weekly trip to the village and I was waiting for you. I walked up and down in the yard and watched the door to the alley, listening for the familiar sound of the key in the lock. Not even a spark of light from the windows dared break the darkness. It was another blackout night.

I knew there were eyes behind the neighbors' drawn curtains. People always want to know the secrets of others. They wanted to find out what was happening in our house, why I had come back from America, what was going on now that my brother had gone out of his mind, abandoning his wife and house. They wanted to know what had happened to my mother, and where I had taken her.

That morning I was delighted—you were coming back from the village after visiting your mother and my mother. I couldn't stay put thinking about you and wanting you to be with me. I went to the garden of Hafezieh and sat beside the poet's tomb. With him alone I shared our secret, reading his poems and whispering that I loved you. Even in this time when love must be hidden, when couples can be stopped by the zealots patrolling the streets because they dare to hold hands or smile or wear clothes that aren't black. Our revolution was not for the earthly pleasures of this life, but the one after—or so we were told. I knew our beloved poet would understand me, because in his time, centuries ago, it was the same—hypocrisy was at its height and lovers had to hide. I walked in the shade of the cypress trees, lost in the hope that someday we could come here freely.

In the afternoon I rushed home to wait for you. It was another Wednesday, those Wednesdays we waited for so impatiently—how slow they were in coming. I waited for you to be in my arms. I would try to take your mind off Ruzbeh and you would help me cope with life in this strange new Iran I'd returned to. You were late, and how impatient I was, wondering if the Jeep had as usual caused more problems on the road or Mother had become hysterical again. Had Ruzbeh run away again or returned more disturbed? I always hoped that he would stay away so you could come to me.

It was almost midnight when I heard the Jeep stop in the alley, and I ran through the courtyard to the door, only to stop short when I heard shouts coming from the alley. My hand dropped as I reached for the latch. I knew you were behind the door, key in hand and scared to death. Only the thin metal was between us and I didn't dare open it. I could hear them questioning you. They were shouting but you kept silent. What could you tell them? That you couldn't speak? That for years you'd been silent? And even if you could have spoken how could you have explained who you were and the reason you were there?

And if I had opened the door, what could I have said?—that you were my sister, my wife, my brother's wife? At a time when a man and woman found together must be married or be brother and sister or mother and son. What could I have done?

I wanted you to be with me like the first time. Like the year before, when you ran to me, threw off your chador and your scarf, your silver bracelets jangling as you used sign language to explain about Ruzbeh, how you waited but he never showed up, and Mother, who went on weeping for him and complaining that you hadn't been a good wife. I saw the tears shining in your green eyes. I opened my arms and you fell into them. We held each other, your head on my shoulder and my lips on your neck. Your hair brushed my face and in spite of my nervousness I could sense your anxiety through your trembling body. This was the closest we'd ever been. I pushed the image of Ruzbeh out of my mind and kissed you. At first you hesitated and pulled away. I waited motionless. It seemed forever before you came back into my arms. We never thought it would be this way, but I was not sorry and could see you felt the same.

For a year, despite all the difficulties we managed to go on and keep our relationship secret. When Ruzbeh came home from his wandering, which happened only once or twice, anxiety and guilt overcame us and we would decide to end our affair. Ruzbeh's well-being was more important to both of us. We took him to doctors and got his prescriptions refilled and made sure he would take his medicine on schedule, but each time, a week or two later we would find the pills in a wastebasket and he would be gone. We knew that he hadn't been able to stop the noises in his head—the bombing, the shelling, and the cries of the wounded that he had heard would haunt him. He had no choice except to walk, he told us, to try and get rid of them that way. We would drive through the streets, in a city of half a million people, looking for him and would argue, accusing each other of wrongdoing and him of not wanting to be helped.

Behruz, go—go back to America, you would write on the pad of paper you always carried for times when communication was difficult. You were disappointed and frustrated with me and said I should go back to my old life and my girlfriends.

I told you I would go back if I could, would try to find a way, but how? Everything is hopeless in this miserable place.

And you would go on saying that you were sorry that I was unhappy, sorry that you wrote with the news of Ruzbeh's being injured in the war and asking me to come back. You thought, you would say, that if one person could help him it was me and how wrong you've been.

I would tell you that the situation wasn't your fault or mine. No one could have anticipated that things would be worse than when you wrote. That I hadn't come back just because you asked, I had my own reasons. I wanted to come back, and I didn't anticipate these problems either. And I, even though embarrassed, would admit my weakness, that I wasn't capable of dealing with all the despair that had come my way and I needed you.

Yes, everything is miserable, you would write down angrily and hand me the paper to read. Yes, it's more miserable for women, but even so, you said that you want to be happy. You wanted to love and live and wouldn't give in to a gradual death that many of us are allowing ourselves to fade into. You wouldn't give in to despair and would fight it no matter what.

You put your finger on my chest, pushed, and said that I had lost hope and that was the worst thing and you couldn't understand that and that I should find a way to go back to America, because the problem of Ruzbeh was yours and you would deal with it yourself and the relationship I was in with you was not good for either of us.

That would be your last comment and a moment later you would be in my arms. But the night you needed me the most, I abandoned you. I ran up to the roof of our house under the cover of the blackout, jumped from roof to roof, and got away. Day after day I wandered around the city looking for you while trying not to raise any suspicions. I heard unkind words spoken about us. I learned that they were searching for me, that they were going to purge the city of people like us.

"Behruz?"

I hear Musa and raise my head. His expression is intense. "Are you all right? Here, have some more tea." He fills up the cup. "I have to go soon. But first I have to tell you a few things. I know you're not well, but this is important and there's not much time." He lights a cigarette. "In the shape you are in, smoking is not good for you or I would offer you a cigarette."

He becomes quiet suddenly and watches the fields through the open door as if trying to track someone's movement.

"If Ruzbeh were here and was well," he says, "this place wouldn't be run down this way. It wouldn't be in danger of being taken over, either. Ah, poor Ruzbeh. It's hard to imagine what war is like, what he went through at the front and then being injured. Even Shireen became strange to him—Shireen whom he loved so much. You weren't here to see them together in this orchard. It was like the Garden of Eden, and they were inseparable. You know, they had plans for this place. Ruzbeh was studying agriculture at the university in Shiraz. Shireen was studying there too, although I'm not sure what. You know all this of course. Ruzbeh told me he was learning about new ways to irrigate the desert. The way the Israelis have done wonders in the Holy Land. He said there were experts coming from Israel to study the irrigation system in our province and that he might go to Israel to see for himself. It would have been a nice trip for him. Israel—I wonder what it's like there. But then everything changed with the revolution. Overnight America and Israel were the enemy. Then the war with Iraq started and Ruzbeh like many young people ended up going to the front."

I don't want him to talk anymore. Everything he says is causing me more anxiety. I wish he would get up and leave as he said he was going to.

"I've looked for him all over," he says, pointing outside. "To the end of the fields and into the desert. What is this 'shell shock' we hear about these days? All these awful new words that we never heard before and now are on our tongues day and night. I can't comprehend the power of a grenade or rocket—a man-made thing that blows people up and even if you're far away, these things still shake you so hard that the sound never goes out of your head. Has God created us to make these sorts of things? Ruzbeh was a calm and free-spirited man before he went to the war and became *moji*—shell-shocked. That's what they call it, shell-shocked. It's something new to us in this country, we never had seen it or heard of it before. Until a few months ago Ruzbeh would come here, sunburned, weak, and lost. Each time, I tried to make him stay. I gave him a big bowl of milk and some *nan* or whatever food I had with me. He ate in silence, although I could see he was nervous. He would eat quickly and then go back to the desert. You know what I think? I think he hears the sounds of the war in his head."

Agitated, I get up and move toward the door. I need to go and find Ruzbeh, but neither my mind nor my body cooperates. I feel light-headed and nauseous.

"What are you doing? You can't go out in this hot wind, in this sun. Sit down." He talks as if he understood my intention. "You won't find him, believe me. We have to wait for him."

I sit down and keep my silence.

"What can I say about these strange times? May God forgive those who pain us, damage us, and do evil acts. Well, what was I going to tell you? Ah, yes. You see, I actually went to the city to try and tell you. And that's when I first heard about Shireen. One of your neighbors told me. I sat there in the alley by your door and cried. Yes, I cried. How could that happen? I told myself it must be a mistake. They must have been looking for someone else. It has happened before that they took away the wrong person. Shireen was intelligent. When she was going to the university, many times she brought her classmates here. I would sit and listen to them and watch Shireen talking to them in sign language. They were full of ideas about everything, eager and hopeful for better days. For sure there must be a mistake.

"Your neighbors told me you'd run away, gone back to America. People have nothing to do these days except talk. Empty talk is as abundant as the sand out there in the desert." He points outside and is quiet for a moment.

"Now that you're here, you must stay put. These days no property should be left without its owner close by. This place belongs to you, to your family. You shouldn't let it run down. This beautiful property could be like the Garden of Eden again, if you take care of it."

I can't help smiling at this hopeful old man and his ridiculous idea.

"I need to be as clear as I can. I've seen some people coming here, looking around. They're just waiting for any excuse to take the property out of your hands. Maybe it's the villagers. But I would say more likely someone from the city. City people have been going around finding places like this and buying them for practically nothing or taking them over, mostly properties that belonged to people who had to leave the country because of the revolution. You see, they can do it because they have connections in the new government. This young man—Kemal is his name—is one of them. He's the one who told me what happened to Shireen. I didn't believe him until I went to Shiraz myself. He's a suspicious young man, if you want my opinion. I think he scared Ruzbeh away, and that's why your brother hasn't come back for months. Kemal seems to be everyone's enemy. I don't know what group or gang he has connections with or what illegal things he has his hands in."

He goes to the door and looks out for a moment.

"I've seen him come here with several other people. I've seen them looking around and wandering in the Naranjestan. I've tried to figure him out, but he's too clever for me. He won't give you a straight answer. If he comes here, which I'm sure he will, you must be very careful. I suspect—no, as a matter of fact, I *know*—that he is after this lemon grove. When you were abroad in America, his father was killed in a fight over land. Someone hit him on the head with a club. For what? For a piece of land, a piece of scorched earth. For a piece of this salt land! How much greed humans have. We forget that in the end all the land we really need is less than six feet! This Kemal has his eye on the land. He's told everyone that he has a share in this place because his father lost his life over it. But that's not true. I know that. It wasn't this land. It was a different property altogether. I've heard him say, 'I'm going to take this place. Aghaye Pirzad's sons are not the type to take care of it. Ruzbeh has lost his mind and is wandering in the desert and Behruz is in the city daydreaming about America.'"

Suddenly Musa gets up and looks outside.

"That's what I wanted to tell you. I owe this much to your parents and to Ruzbeh. They've always helped me and my family. If you hang around, I may be willing to tell you more one of these days. It's too much for one day. Now it's up to you. This place is yours—it belongs to your family. You're here now, not in America."

He picks up his stick. "Don't think of doing anything crazy. And don't leave this room."

I try to smile at him as he turns and goes out. I go to the door and watch until he is no longer visible in the dusk and it's as if he'd become one with the desert.

Four

I CAN'T REMEMBER FALLING ASLEEP last night, but my first night's sleep in days left my mind calmer. Early this morning, when I went to the orchard to urinate, my urine was bloody. I wasn't alarmed, but the sharp burning brought tears to my eyes. I haven't told the old man, having no patience for his remedies.

Yesterday Musa brought another old army blanket and a kerosene lamp. He helped me move to a different room of the farmhouse. This room is much cleaner and has two windows. From one of the windows I can see the well and the redbrick pump house next to it. A pipe from the pump leads from the pump house to a small cement pool, now empty and only dreaming of the *shor-shor* of flowing water. Beyond the pump house, the fields spread out flat as far as the village, about four miles distant. The desert-colored village is often barely visible except for the smoke that coils up mornings and afternoons.

Through the east window are the trees of the Naranjestan, half of them dead now and in need of replacement. Many times when we stayed in this room, Ruzbeh would wake me to see the morning sun over the white blossoms. The lemon grove covers about fifty acres and has a single row of sycamore trees as a border around it. In the distance, the arid mountains stretch southward with the ancient city of Shiraz hidden in the valley behind—is it possible that Shireen is still there?

The wind is blowing continually. It blows with determination, as if trying to summon up the wandering ghosts of this ancient land and scatter them to the far corners of the earth. It sweeps over the orchard and fields, picking up dust and dead leaves and rolling them up into whirlwinds that glide across the land. As soon as one reaches the edge of the desert, another picks up. One after another they circle over the fields, taking their gatherings and wrapping them up in an amber veil of dust and thorns rising up to the sun.

The bare, half-dead trees of the orchard are in a fearful battle with the wind. They bow and bend and every so often a branch breaks away, light and empty, giving way to the flow.

This ruined farmhouse and everything else I see around me are not the way I remember. The house has been added on to and has a new hallway with three more rooms. There's a stone porch in front with columns, now crumbing, that hold up the roof. Nearby there is a half-finished swimming pool. Maybe this is what Ruzbeh meant in his letter when he said he was building a place as nice as any I had seen in America. I still remember his words—"Behruz-*aziz,* the beauty of a place is not only in fair weather and greenery. The pleasant company of friends is a must as well. When you come back, we will flee the heat and gloom of the city with our friends and come here. We'll stay all summer if we want. Like our childhood days—you must remember."

Remember? Certainly I remember. You weren't aware of what was happening to me—how I waited for your letters and how with each one I would imagine you and Shireen in the gardens of Shiraz or in the Naranjestan, talking and laughing. And now, everywhere I look, I see you, Ruzbeh. I see you, Shireen, and remember the times we wanted to love and be loved.

In springtime we were happy. Even Father was glad to leave the city and the calamities of his office behind, and Mother couldn't wait to get to the orchard and into the open air. She enjoyed being with Shireen's mother and loved Shireen as if she were her own daughter. We would run into the Naranjestan among the trees and crimson-flowered poppies. Father would sit at his usual place under the willow tree, smoking his water pipe, drinking tea, and watching the workers in the orchard. Sometimes he would sit there for hours, maybe daydreaming about the grandchildren who someday would be there playing around him.

The spring days would be quiet with the orchard full of lemon flowers and the fields green with winter wheat. Then one day the blossoms would wither and cover the ground. Father would order Haji Zaman to organize another round of fumigation. People would come to look, talk, and gossip and would offer all sorts of opinions. Someone would say it was the water, another would claim it was the soil or the fertilizer. There was even whispering that it was the wrongdoing of our ancestors!

The government agricultural technicians came too. They would wander in the lemon grove collecting branches and soil samples and then suggest a particular treatment—every year something different, but with the same results. Nothing improved. And you, Ruzbeh, you also fought the diseases and even went to school to study agriculture. You tried to send soil samples to me in America, unaware that U.S. law forbids the entrance of soil or seeds.

Haji Zaman would try to convince the concerned people, even the agricultural technicians, that it was the work of demons and jinnis. He would ask Mother to walk with his wife through the orchard, carrying a Koran and burning incense in an effort to send the ancient ghosts back to the desert. We would follow behind, chanting along with childish seriousness. We listened quietly as Mother talked to the trees, telling them to get well and touching them to see if they had a fever. And now, here they are, the old trees still hanging on despite the endless years of drought.

Father died two years after I went away to America, but when I look toward where he used to sit beside the dry stream, I can almost see his bony figure. He's stooped over and sucking on the empty water pipe, his hands like dry branches, his eyes as empty as the fields in front of him. His voice, though, is strong, as it was even in old age. "There's no hope for you, Behruz," he says. "You're here and not here. You don't stay and you don't go away. You're happy and not happy. You have your heart here and God knows where else. Look at you! I foresaw your future very clearly. I knew you weren't patient enough to finish anything. Why did you go to America with a heart full of hopes and dreams and then return to this scorched land? Someone like you isn't made for taking care of this place. Leave it, go away from here."

But you, Ruzbeh, you were his man. You became his man. He grew to trust you, to believe in you. He knew you would take care of this place, keep it alive. And you did what you could. You were able to do it because you had Shireen beside you. Did you know, Ruzbeh, that I left to give you room to be with Shireen? You had the benefit of her beauty and high spirits, her strength and hopefulness to help you take care of the old orchard until the hurricane of revolution came, uprooting the established order and replacing it by force with a new and unexpected one. A cataclysmic change that gave birth to the war that has been devastating for you and so many others.

Tired of standing and looking through the window, I go outside. I shield my eyes from the wind and see a shadowlike movement in the haze. It must be Musa and his sheep out in the fields. I wander in the orchard and stop under a sycamore tree where Father put a rope over a big branch and made a swing. What an unforgettable day we had here, a day that left its ugliness with you, Shireen. We were only children. We were only playing.

The three of us were here in the corner of the orchard. We had tied a white chador to the trees and made a tent, a bridal chamber, and acted out a wedding, our own made-up wedding. You were the bride, Ruzbeh the groom. I was a friend invited to the wedding. I can see it now. We were lying down with you between us. I was holding you from one side and Ruzbeh from the other. It was a warm, nice feeling, just lying together, enjoying our innocent game. The sun and the shadows of the branches were playing on the top of the chamber, when suddenly a voice came like thunder, the birds scattered, and the chamber was pulled away.

"What are you doing? Who taught you this?" It was Haji Zaman. "It's all your idea, Shireen, isn't it?" He grabbed your hand, yanked you up, and wrapped the chador around you. "I can see it in those devilish eyes of yours!"

I could feel his grip around my wrist, pulling me up. He bent over, looking straight at you. "You wretched girl. You're always up to something shameful, aren't you? What were you doing? Ha! Tell me!"

Ruzbeh got up and stood beside you. I didn't understand what was wrong, what we had done that was so bad. Haji looked at me with his big red eyes, then at Ruzbeh. I cried, "Maman, Maman," but you didn't cry and didn't answer your stepfather. Ruzbeh was holding your other hand. Between my tears I saw Haji's hand going up and then coming down.

"What were you doing?" he shouted. *Slap.* "Ha? Tell me." *Slap.* "Or by Allah I'll cut your tongue out."

He bent down in front of you. "If you do things like this now, what will you do when you grow up?"

Then I saw my mother and your mother rush toward us as if flying. I ran to Mother's open arms, but Ruzbeh stood there holding your hand.

"Why are you hitting the children?" Mother said angrily.

"They are doing shameful things." Haji Zaman raised his voice. "It's all Shireen's idea. She must be punished. I can't touch these boys. But her—she must learn not to do it again."

"Haji, don't hit my child," your mother said, stepping closer to wrest your hand from Haji's grip.

He pushed her away. "Tell me, Shireen!" he demanded. "It was your idea, wasn't it?"

He dragged you toward the pump house. Ruzbeh didn't let go of your hand and was pulled along.

"Haji, let the child go," Mother pleaded.

"No, Khanom. No. I've got to punish her. If I don't do it now, I'll never be able to control her later."

Haji stopped by the fire that he had fed with the dry brush and branches he had collected throughout the Naranjestan. I watched as you clenched your teeth while trying to free your wrist from Haji's grip. Suddenly he screamed. You had one of his fingers between your teeth.

"You bite me, ha? You don't want to talk, ha? I'll make you talk."

I saw the flames of the fire and the reddened tongs in Haji's hand. With his other hand he was trying to open your mouth.

"Haji, don't. Don't hurt my child," your mother asked desperately, pulling Haji's coat. "I swear to Allah, don't hurt my child. Let her go!"

Haji pushed her away.

"I knew it," your mother wailed from the ground. "I knew you would never be a father to her. Oh, did God take her father away from me so I would end up with this cruel man?" She grabbed Haji's leg.

"Don't, Haji," said Mother, holding Haji's arm. "Don't do it," she said, struggling with him. Haji finally managed to free himself. Then I saw you flat on the ground with Ruzbeh bent down, still holding your hand, and Haji Zaman moving away.

I listen and then hear the sound of a motorcycle. On the path from the village dust is rising and a motorcycle is coming toward the Naranjestan. I hurry back to the house and look out the window. The tails of the bandana tied around the rider's head flap out behind him. He slows down and stops by the pump house. He is a slim man with a mustache and is wearing olive-green clothes.

When he takes off his sunglasses and looks toward the window, I squat down, hoping he won't see me. The few minutes that pass seem like forever. Then I hear voices. I move behind the door and try to see through the broken boards. The cyclist talks to Musa, then grabs an old shovel lying beside the building and walks to the orchard.

Musa hurries into the room and gestures to me not to make a sound. I watch the man, a ghostly figure in the dust and wind, digging beneath one of the lemon trees.

"That's Kemal," Musa whispers, "the young man I told you about."

Kemal takes a small sack out of the hole and shakes off the dirt. Then he throws down the shovel and walks toward the house. I freeze and don't know what I should do or could do. Before Kemal gets any closer, Musa runs out to meet him. They talk for a moment and then turn and together walk back toward the motorcycle. Kemal ties the sack on the back of the motorcycle and, pointing to the house, says something to Musa. I turn my head and try to hear them, but the wind takes their voices away.

Musa waves his hand toward the building, then toward the desert, pointing at something or indicating a direction. Giving up on trying to understand, I drop to the dirt floor, my heart beating hard against the ground.

Five

THE SPOT BESIDE THE DRY STREAM has become my favorite place. I sit against a half-dead tree and watch the fields and the village in the distance. If I see anyone coming this way, I can disappear into the lemon grove.

There is a group of men, women, and children on the road and it looks like they have emerged from a long-forgotten world. They carry black-and-green banners that wave above their heads. The beating of the drums and the mourning wails are just like in a passion play. The women are in black cloaks that shimmer in the bright sunlight. A fawn-colored horse is being led at the front of the group. The horse, Musa says, is named Zoljena after the horse of Imam Hossein who fought against the infidels in the desert of Karbala. The animal is kept saddled and ready for the Holy War against the new Iraqi infidels. I don't know how many times I've looked out at a scene like this. Maybe every day since I came here—I've lost count. They are probably on their way to the city to accompany the young men going to the front or to bring the body of a martyr back home.

It was past midnight when I finally fell asleep. As on all the other nights I dreamed of the square in the city and the chanting crowd that was hunting me. I couldn't see their faces, only their dark figures, shadowy in the bright daylight. Their pockets were full and their hands ready as they waited for the casting of the first stone. In the square a figure wrapped in a white shroud was buried to her bosom.

The shrieks of the jackals woke me. I could hear them beyond the walls of the farmhouse. They have been coming out every night, and in the mornings I've seen their footprints on the soft ground around the building. This morning, at dawn when they were gone and the horizon was turning to amber, I ventured out half-asleep and went into the orchard. The trees were still, as if resting from their night's battle with the wind. For a moment I thought I saw someone moving behind the trees. Although fearful, I looked around, thinking it could be Ruzbeh. I walked out of the orchard and still didn't see anyone. I kept walking until I reached the desert and the sand, cool from the night's chill, grew warm under my feet. I tore my shirt off my parched skin and went on. I walked until the sun was directly above me in a colorless sky. My feet burned from the desert salt that had crept into every cut. My mouth was dry, and I felt the sand scratching my throat. Around me dead bushes whispered in the wind.

But where did I go? And how did I get back to the Naranjestan? Was it a human figure I saw there in the distance, or only a shimmering shadow, a trick of the desert? Was someone watching me from afar? If it was Ruzbeh, why did he run away from me? I walked in his direction, but each time I got closer he was gone. I have to go on searching this unsearchable place until I find him. I have to tell him what happened to Shireen—he needs to know. I should go back to the city and search for him and Shireen. Maybe she is alive. Maybe she survived. Could it be possible to survive the anger and the stones? Maybe she too ran away to the desert. Maybe we're all here in this desert full of the signs and secrets of defeated and victorious people and dynasties come and gone.

Last evening I watched the full moon slowly rise and roll out her silver sheets over the desert. But then she went away, as if there were somewhere else she had to be. Left alone in the night, I lay down on the brick platform beside the farmhouse and listened to the desert—

the sounds that come alive in the dark, the whispers that move past as if the earth were breathing.

I wandered lost among the stars and the darkness. The flickering stars reminded me of the fireflies that I saw with Juanita those summer evenings in America. I went to the United States to study. But I couldn't sit and listen to the math instructor with a voice like chalk on a blackboard, or the chemistry teacher whose hair and eyebrows looked like he had stood too close to the Bunsen burner, or the beginning-philosophy professor with his bushy mustache, trying to look like Nietzsche. Why couldn't I concentrate on my studies? What went wrong? Was it as Father always said—that I didn't know what I wanted and didn't take the time to finish one thing before starting something else? Or was it pure laziness and confusion at being on my own? I was too willing to leave my classes and go traveling. To be in a larger classroom, as I thought then, to travel that vast, open land laced with rivers and fertile with forests and fields. To see the cities that scratch the arc of the sky, full of people from the far corners of the globe.

If it hadn't been for my friend Juanita, I wouldn't have had a chance to see the Great Plains. She was a Native American and had jet-black hair hanging down to her waist and an energetic and easygoing nature. She liked to laugh and knew how to deal with the sense of dislocation I often felt in America. I miss the days that we drove to different states and wandered through the downtowns of American cities. We would go to a movie theater—here they're all burned down—or to a play—something that hardly exists now in Iran. After the theater we would go for a drink at a jazz club. If only I were back in a noisy and smoky bar with Juanita, our heads dizzy with cold beer and hot conversation.

I promised Juanita that we would go to Iran to experience the desert nights in the Naranjestan and be with Ruzbeh and Shireen. I showed her the letters I had from Shireen when she was studying sociology at the university. She sent news of a campus tense with postrevolutionary changes. Conservative Islamists were ordering women to wipe off their makeup and cover their heads and men not to wear short-sleeve shirts, but the socialists and liberal students and professors were fighting back. Many of the leftist and liberal faculty were being purged from their jobs. Students were boycotting classes and marching on behalf of their professors. Women were standing strong to demand that civil family law not be changed to religious law and that wearing *hijab* should not be a demand but a choice. In one letter Shireen described how she and her friend Farideh were participating in the movement and gone to the International Women's Day in Tehran to march with more than a million protesters, mostly women, cheering and demanding equality. The American feminist Kate Millett had traveled to Tehran to support the protesters, marching in the front line of the demonstration. The Islamists were there too, to disrupt the march and enforce *hijab*. Women without chadors or scarves were beaten up and Kate Millett was detained for three days before being expelled from the country— Juanita and I saw the event on the ABC evening news.

I used to dream of having Shireen and Ruzbeh come to America so they could experience the freedom there. Then we would be a family again. I knew they would both like Juanita. There were so many things we could show them. Well, they tried. They got their visas and their tickets, only to be unable to follow their plan, because the American Embassy in Tehran was seized by Islamists and the embassy personnel were taken hostage. Shortly after, all diplomatic ties between Iran and the United States were cut.

In the years just before the revolution, I had endless arguments with my Iranian friends about the political situation in Iran. The Shah's totalitarian regime controlled the media and didn't tolerate any opposing voice. One-party rule and the sword of censorship hung above the heads of writers and intellectuals and halted our progress toward democracy. In private we argued and debated. Some of us believed that class struggle would pave the way for an urban guerrilla movement as in Cuba. Some denounced the armed struggle altogether. We spent hours trying to grasp the meaning of concepts like "surplus value." The Trotskyites and Stalinists were always at one another's throats. The Islamic students denounced all of us.

It was a time of words, hopes, and illusions. One friend would talk of "Permanent Revolution," another would bring up thesis, antithesis, and synthesis no matter the subject, except that he would say it in a different order each time, not really understanding the concept.

Yet another friend would attend the meetings wearing boots and overalls, believing that a true revolutionary must be close to the proletarian way of life—he even slept in these clothes to show his sympathy with the working class, since, according to him, in capitalist societies workers didn't even have time to sleep normally. This was the same friend who owned a black Trans Am that he would drive through the streets of downtown trying to impress the girls.

We organized demonstrations, sympathized with other international students, Latin American, Palestinian, and African, and tried to denounce capitalism and be the voice of any social movement around the world. Our rallies always attracted a few Vietnam veterans with shabby army jackets and long hair. We had the dream that one day we would have a country without political prisoners or torture, where there was hope for the future, and we were eager to go back and lend a hand. America was the battleground of growing up for me, a world that I wanted to become a part of but couldn't embrace totally. I knew I could never completely free myself from Iran. I missed it and was always thinking of my family. It was as if I were suspended between two worlds. The easygoing world of being a student in the United States and the complex culture and habits I grew up with in Iran that were so slow in loosening their hold on me.

My memories of Juanita calm me down and help me to deal with the loneliness that is always present within me. She comes to me, to my arms. She brings me quietness, the way she always did in our small apartment filled with plants in that small midwestern town where I would lie beside her on the cold nights of winter. She would tell me stories about her Indian ancestors who roamed the plains from the Dakotas to Oklahoma. I would tell her of the orchard of sweet Persian lemons.

"Sweet lemons?"

"Yes, sweet ones. They're yellow just like the ones here, but sweet. We have an orchard called Naranjestan. In spring the lemon grove would be in full blossom, and I would be there with my brother and Shireen—her name means sweet, too."

"Who was Shireen?"

I felt a lump in my throat, not knowing what to say. Not being able to say that she was my brother's girlfriend but that I liked her too.

"She's married to my brother now. I would love to have them meet you. Maybe someday we'll go there."

Maybe. It was "maybe" that controlled my life. Maybe I should stay in the United States and forget about everything back home. Maybe I should just go back to Iran. Maybe, maybe, maybe. It was a plague of uncertainty and doubt. Then came the revolution, a revolution derailed by the Islamists with their anti-Americanism and hostage-taking. And then the war. Not long after Ruzbeh had been called to the front, I received a letter from Shireen saying that he had been injured. I had to make a decision, but my mind was clouded with anger at the war and the people who had brought it about. Not knowing at all what to do disturbed me, and the result of it was arguing with Juanita. Everything seemed to unleash itself against our euphoria. She wanted me to wait and think about the future. But the future was dark to me. I could only think of my brother. Juanita came to doubt my love for her. I decided I had to go back and spent the fourteen-hour flight home sitting without speaking to anyone.

Those first few months, I thought of her constantly.

Dear Juanita,

I'm sending you
this letter from Persia
with the smell of tea and tangerines.
The tea is hot and the tangerine
is peeled beside my bed.

Make a pot of hot tea, peel
a cool tangerine beside your bed.
Imagine my kisses
with the bitterness of tea
and sweetness of the tangerine
as I imagine yours.

Behruz

I WAS LYING ON THE PLATFORM and must have been dozing when I heard footsteps. I opened my eyes and saw a man in sunglasses standing there watching me. He was stroking his mustache and grinning. I sat up quickly. I recognized him. He was Kemal, the man that Musa warned me about, and there was no time to walk away.

"I didn't hear your motorcycle," I said, trying not to show my nervousness.

"Exactly," he said, taking off his glasses. "That's why you see me in front of you. If you had heard it you would have been heading into the orchard like every other time. I parked it away from here and walked."

"What can I do for you?" I asked apprehensively.

"Nothing." He sat on the edge of the platform. "There's nothing I want. I just like to come here once in a while. That's all. To get away."

I didn't trust his calm demeanor and remained on guard. "I see. I'm Behruz Pirzad. This is my property."

"I know who you are." He smiled. "You don't need to be alarmed. I'm Kemal."

I didn't say anything. He smoothed his mustache, staring at me. "Ruzbeh and I were friends. I used to come here often."

"He's not here now."

"I know. I wish he were. This place needs him."

"Did you work for him?"

"Not really, I came by when he had a problem with the motor pump. The last thing I did was to help him build the pool that never got finished."

I must have appeared nervous because he said again that I didn't need to be alarmed. That he knew Ruzbeh and Shireen very well. And that at one point Ruzbeh had wanted him to work for him. But he didn't want to because at the time he had a good job at the oil refinery on the road to Shiraz and was planning to move to the city.

"Why were you helping him?" I asked impatiently.

He stared at me in disbelief. "Why? Because he's my friend . . . It seems you don't trust me. I've always tried to do what I can for him. I've taken my motorcycle into the desert many times looking for him."

He talked rapidly as if he had to be somewhere. He was quiet for a moment, then suddenly got up, put on his sunglasses, and hurried away. I was surprised to find myself wishing that he hadn't left so suddenly. I wanted to find out what he knew about Ruzbeh, whether he had ever seen him around here.

The next day, sitting in my usual spot, I watched the road and waited. I thought he would do the same thing—park his bike far away and walk. He didn't come that day, but on the third day I heard the motorcycle. He came right up to the pump house, parked, and drew water from the well. After washing up he came to the platform, carrying a shoulder bag.

"I have a few things for you," he said, opening the bag. "I thought you could keep yourself entertained with what goes on in this country." He handed me a couple of magazines and newspapers. "Although you can't trust what you read in them."

"Thanks," I said warily.

"I'm glad you didn't try to avoid me this time."

"Should I have?"

"No. There's no reason to. I couldn't believe it when I heard you'd come back from America. What a time to be back!" He sat down next to me. "Tell me about America."

I was more interested in finding out about Ruzbeh than talking about America, especially to him.

"When was the last time you saw Ruzbeh?" I asked.

"Oh, long ago. At least six months ago."

"Here?"

"No. In Shiraz, at the end of the bazaar, close to the Shah-e-Cheragh shrine. I remember it well, because it was the mourning day for some imam, I don't know which one, and many pilgrims from the countryside were rushing to the shrine. I don't know why Ruzbeh was there or why I was there for that matter, I usually avoid those places. It was like he didn't recognize me or didn't want to acknowledge me. We said hello and he walked away."

"You didn't see him after that?"

"No." He changed the subject yet again. "I'm surprised you came back from America. You must have found everything different from when you went away. It's worse than even a year ago. No jobs, no security. People have changed too. In this time and place you have to be clever. If you're not more clever than the next guy, he'll take your shirt off your back. Trust no one these days. If you ask people around here about me, everyone will tell you something different. Don't believe everything you hear. What people say doesn't bother me a bit. Most of them can't even see what's in front of their nose. Don't get me wrong. Musa's not like that. He's a decent man. He has been looking after this place since Ruzbeh went away."

"I know," I said.

He grabbed his bag. "A few times I asked Musa to let me fix the motor pump and try to irrigate the lemon grove, which is dying of thirst, or just grow some vegetables for our own use. Each time his answer was, 'The permission has to come from Pirzad's family.'"

He eyed me expectantly. "Now that you're here, it could come from you." Then he raised his hand in a half salute. "See you later."

Seven

TODAY IN THE DESERT I FOUND MYSELF near an ancient ruin with toppled columns and statues of winged bulls buried in the sand. There was a frieze with an animal standing on its hind legs—a demon in the shape of a winged bull. A warrior was grabbing the bull's horn and pushing his sword into its body up to the hilt. It was obvious from the crown on the warrior's head that he was a majestic king. Maybe it was a belief of the time that a king had to prove his bravery by confronting a creature from the underworld.

I wished I knew whether the king was clenching his jaws in anger or wearing a victorious smile. I guess he was smiling, since, centuries later, another conqueror—one who had perhaps forbidden smiling even on the faces of statues—had scratched out his face. I touched the disfigured face, thinking of this ancient land and all the victories and defeats it has seen. Then out of the corner of my eye I saw a shadow moving among the broken rubble. Was someone watching me? I rushed away, but nothing was visible in the midday haze when I looked back. There was only a soft sound of bells jingling in the distance. I ran until I was back at the Naranjestan, my feet full of cuts and thorns.

People say that in ancient times this land had forests and wild animals and was the hunting ground for kings and princes. A branch of the Silk Road passed nearby leading west to Arabia and east to Samarkand. The ruins of caravansaries still mark the route. Did I read it somewhere, or was it Musa who told me about the ruins of a palace out in the desert? A palace that shows itself only to certain people. If you have the destiny to see it, or so the story goes, no one knows what it will do to you. It's said that people have come out of the desert, their hair having turned totally white or having lost their minds or gone blind, but some ended up becoming wise and even rich. Around here these stories blow with the wind.

I don't believe all the tales that people tell, but on the other hand, that is what the desert does to you if you stay too long—you start to doubt the truth and believe the false. Did I see the palace or was it another trick of the desert? I wonder what Musa knows and isn't saying. Maybe I'll go back and look again. Maybe it was the ruin of the palace that Musa told me about. The glass palace with a mirror that could show the future. Maybe I could find a piece of the mirror.

I return to the Naranjestan exhausted and stretch out on the platform beside the farmhouse. It's late afternoon and Musa is driving his herds to the well. Two goats run to the well ahead of the rest and at the same time thrust their heads into the empty water bucket, and as they keep pushing it, their horns bang against the metal. The sheep, numbering around a dozen, stand together patiently, their heads low, each trying to hold its head in the shade of another. Their round bellies move up and down as they breathe. The smell of wool, urine, and dung fills the air. Musa walks over to the platform, throws down his walking stick, and sits in the shade of the wall.

"This heat is after me or my herds," he says, breathing heavily. "It's like fire pouring from the earth and sky. I've never seen such heat."

He takes off his hat and rubs his head, then wipes his face and the back of his neck with a handkerchief. He hasn't rested for long when he gets up and walks to the edge of the well, taking the bucket the goats have abandoned and lowering it. Hearing the sound, the animals rush toward him. He yanks at the rope a few times to make the bucket fill before pulling it up. Water pours from the holes of the banged-up bucket. The animals circle him, trying to shove their heads in. He pushes a few away and holds them while two by two they drink. "Hold on a second," he says, "easy, easy, let her finish first. You creatures are just like humans, greedy and selfish." He draws water several times until the last animal is satisfied. Then he throws the bucket down the well once more and calls out to me.

"Come and cool yourself down."

I watch him wash his hands and face. Even though sweat is running down my face, I don't feel like moving. My shirt is like a piece of old leather, and my skin is sunburned and flakes off when I rub it. I'm used to all that now, used to my rough beard and smelling of earth and desert.

"It'll cool you down," he says.

I get up and walk to the well. I've never liked to go close to it, even in my childhood days. It has always scared me—a mysterious circular hole that could suck you into the heart of the earth. It's at least twelve feet across and the low cement wall around it is about two feet high. Standing at the edge, I stretch my neck out cautiously and look down at the dark surface of the water. I don't know how deep it is—twenty feet perhaps. It was dug out God knows when. As far back as I remember it has been here. Father had a plan to abandon it and have a drilled well with a better pump. His thinking was that the disease of the Naranjestan was from the old well.

Musa pours water on my hands as I rub them together and wash. The cool water tickles my skin as it runs down my neck and back. I pull off my shirt and wash it out. Before going back to the shade, I wash my feet. The cuts and bruises start to burn. I go back on the platform and stretch out on the kilim. Musa brings some brush from the orchard to build a small fire for his water pipe and boil water for tea. He fills the pipe with water from the bucket and tosses what's left on the mud bricks of the sitting platform, causing the smell of damp earth to rise. From a plastic bag he takes out two handfuls of crushed tobacco that he puts in the bowl of the water pipe and tamps down with his thumb. I enjoy watching this sturdy, patient man, so efficient and confident in everything he does. He functions like clockwork—coming here, watering his animals, smoking, taking a nap, all a natural and enjoyable routine to him. I disrupted all this in the first days I was here, but it's obvious he has settled back to his usual routine, adding in the things he does for me. When the fire is ready he puts a few tiny embers on top of the tobacco and carries the pipe to the shade, sitting down with crossed legs, his back to the wall.

With the sound of bubbling water and the pleasant smell of burning tobacco, my eyelids start to get heavy.

"Do you remember I said you should never trust this fellow Kemal?" Musa says, and I open my eyes. Not having slept well last night and after wandering in the desert, I was starting to fall into a deep sleep.

"Please listen to me carefully and I'll tell you why," he goes on after sucking on the pipe and letting a billow of smoke rush out of his mouth. "Kemal hasn't done me any harm, let me say that first. But this man may be involved in whatever you can point your finger at. Dangerous deeds. I've heard this from the villagers—you know how they talk. He is always going to Shiraz. Sometimes he disappears for days. What for? Nobody knows.

"But I think I know, and he tries to hide it from me. You shouldn't be fooled by his attentions to you, by his bringing you books or newspapers or vodka from the black market." The smoke rushing out of his nostrils covers his face momentarily. "And I don't know what he's been telling you, but all that is not my business. What concerns me, and for certain should concern you, is what I told you a bit about before. I couldn't say much then, because you weren't well. He has his eyes on this property, on the Naranjestan. That's the thing that's got to do with us. With you, I should say—who am I to include myself? Your parents and Ruzbeh did a lot for me. Actually your father protected my father from the wrath of the villagers. He was a city man who ended up living here because of a love affair. Love—love can become the source of many problems."

He stares at me with his one eye for a long time before continuing. "Maybe one of these days I'll tell you more about my father.

I'm obliged to your parents for their kindness, and to Ruzbeh and Shireen, and I feel sad and disturbed for the lemon grove. My heart aches for Ruzbeh, who worked so hard for this place. During the revolution, when some of the villagers were after the orchard, he fought them back. Shireen was beside him, always." He becomes quiet for a moment. "Shireen was a brave woman. Not afraid of anything. She stayed here and faced the villagers. I myself saw her, stick in hand. You know that she couldn't talk after what happened to her when she was little—I don't need to tell you that—but she stood up to them all the same. At any rate, there were villagers that respected and liked Ruzbeh and Shireen. They must have been able to calm the attackers down."

"You know I liked it the way Shireen talked with her hands. I would stand and watch her and Ruzbeh, talking without saying a word, just gesturing hands moving so fast. Human beings are so fascinating! Sign language, they call it, right? Do you know it too?"

I nod and my heart wrings, thinking about Shireen.

"You know what? At that time Kemal never came here. He wasn't part of the group who were trying to take this place."

He fixes his eye in the distance and sucks on the pipe again.

"May God forgive those who do unforgivable deeds . . . I'm trying to make you see what is going on here. Kemal believes that his father lost his life for this place. Do you remember I told you that his father was killed? He was killed in a fight over land—he was hit with a club on the head. God rest his soul. Kemal's father was an aggravating man, sticking his nose in everyone's business, but he wasn't killed over the Naranjestan. It was over Mansor Khan's land. I don't know exactly what happened, but at the time of the revolution, the time of lawlessness, Mansor Khan was trying to expand his farm onto his neighbor's land. He had brought a tractor and started to plow the land next to his. The neighbor gathered a few people, including Kemal's father, to stop him. A fight broke out and Kemal's father was killed.

Kemal is like his father, but his animosity toward your family is over something else. He was burned by something else, and badly. Although it was years ago, he hasn't forgotten it."

The water pipe bubbles violently as he sucks on the tube and smoke rushes out all around him. I'm not really interested in what he's telling me. I just want to close my eyes and go to sleep.

"You weren't here then," he says. "You had gone to America. Kemal wanted to marry Shireen."

He stares at me with his one eye, waiting to see my reaction. I remember that Shireen wrote to me at the time about this without mentioning the man's name. So it was Kemal. I don't say anything and keep quiet to hear what the old man has to say.

"Haji Zaman, Shireen's stepfather, was dead and Bibi, her mother, wouldn't do anything without your parents' advice. But no matter what Kemal did or said or whom he sent to ask for her hand, it didn't work out. Shireen herself didn't want it. She had been in love with your brother from a young age—I suppose that from childhood they were in love. She was going to school and knew what she wanted. She wasn't going to come back and live in the village again. Maybe you know all this already. Who knows what Kemal has done against Ruzbeh and Shireen? If you ask me, he may be the cause of Ruzbeh's running away. And the hateful things that were done to Shireen? May God never forgive him if he had anything to do with that. As God is my witness, I've only heard this from people talking. I heard that two people from the village and some of your neighbors in the city went with . . ."—he hesitates for a moment—"went with Kemal to a mullah to testify that Shireen had given up her husband . . ." He gazes out at the fields for a moment, and then looks at me. ". . . and stayed alone with you at home—you know what I mean . . ."

Suddenly I sit up in anger and stare at him as he goes on sucking on his water pipe, his face curtained momentarily behind the smoke. I turn my eyes to the fields. I want to get up and go find Kemal. I want to wrap my fingers around his neck until he tells me the truth. Until he tells me if he had anything to do with what happened to Shireen.

"Calm down," Musa says softly. "Calm down. It could be pure gossip. Only God knows. No one can trust what people say. These days you can't even trust your own eyes. These days people are like the desert." He points toward the horizon. "You see water out there? No, it's only sand and heat."

He puts more embers on the pipe and fans it with his hand.

"Sit and listen to me. I know you can't believe what I'm saying. I've only heard the villagers talk. Empty talk, you know. There is too much empty talk these days. You probably can't believe that Kemal could be that cruel. I can't either. But the past is past, and we can't do anything about it. What we need to do is prevent bad things from happening when we can. We need to do everything we can to find Ruzbeh. What I'm saying is that you should be careful and not be fooled by Kemal's bringing vodka or books or who knows what. I believe he knows what he's doing. He has connections with bad people. And I think everything he does is to get this land."

I don't want to listen. I don't care who wants this orchard or who is conspiring to steal it or whether there is any hope for it to survive. Maybe someday someone will take care of it. But it's not going to be me. Or Ruzbeh. Right now I don't care if it's all swept away by the wind. Maybe that would be for the best, the way that everything here has been on a path of destruction. I think of Shireen and look at my hands and my fingers. Bones, muscles, and nerves—the result of millions of years of evolution. I stare at my thumb, the way it curves to the center of my palm to grasp something. I stare at my arm, amazed to think how it could move in a perfect half circle to throw a stone.

Eight

WHEN WE HEAR THE SOUND OF Kemal's motorcycle approaching, Musa stops talking and looks at me for a moment. "Don't do anything foolish," he says and then goes back to smoking his water pipe.

I watch Kemal, trying to control my anger. He parks his motorcycle beside the pump house and walks to the well.

I want to go and look straight into his eyes and ask him, "What did you have to do with what happened to Shireen?" I want to see past his smiling face and calm gestures and find out what is behind those black eyes. I need to find out whether he is the friend he pretends to be. Whether he rode his motorcycle through the desert to find Ruzbeh as he says or whether he scared him away.

I watch as he shakes the dust off his clothes and unties the handkerchief wrapped around his forehead. He throws the bucket down the well and yanks it up quickly. Then he takes off his sunglasses, kneels down, and plunges his head inside the bucket, staying there for such a long time I think he's going to drown. Then with a sudden movement he takes his head out and shakes it right and left, sending drops of water flying.

I close my eyes for a moment, trying in vain to gather my thoughts. When I open them I see him walking toward us. He comes to the platform and shakes his head again, letting droplets of water rain on us.

"Stop it," Musa yells. "You're putting my pipe out."

But Kemal, still shaking his head, takes another step closer. Musa grumbles and shields the top of the water pipe with his hand, sucking harder in an effort to save the burning embers.

Kemal laughs and jumps up onto the platform. "What's the matter, old man?" he says. "Don't let me stop you. You can go on talking about me." His loud laughter makes me jump.

"Here we go . . . ," Musa says. "I thought I was going to have a quiet afternoon, and who comes along to destroy it? The Devil himself."

To my surprise, Kemal doesn't answer him. He squats against the wall and silently watches the fields, then suddenly gets up and walks to the well. There is an uneasiness about him, a restlessness, as if he is waiting for something to happen.

I watch him, my mind clouded by what Musa has been telling me. I don't know what to believe. It occurs to me that they could be talking behind my back and deciding what they should tell me. It would be easy to take advantage of my silence since I hear only their sides of things and never put a question to them.

I wonder if there is any truth to Musa's suspicion of Kemal. Did he really try to harm Shireen by going to the mullah? Did he do it for the land? If he was after the Naranjestan, why didn't he make a move during the first years of the revolution when anarchy ruled the country and people in the rural areas were seizing land from the landowners? A few days after we met, he opened up and talked to me as if I were his best friend. He said that he helped Ruzbeh and Shireen when the villagers tried to take the Naranjestan. Now I doubt his sincerity in encouraging me to look for Ruzbeh and his promise to help to rebuild this place. I wish there were a way to know the truth in all of this. I feel tired and am aching. I think my illness is not getting any better. Not only is my body exhausted but my mind as well, and I can't seem to do anything or think straight and figure out what is going on around here.

Kemal pulls off his shirt and pants and walks to the edge of the well. I watch him, wondering what he is up to. He lowers the bucket down and then grabs the rope and disappears into the mouth of the well as quickly as if he'd never been standing there. My eyes are still on the well, not believing what I've seen, when I hear the faint sound of splashing water.

"It's his habit," Musa says. "I've never seen anything like it in my long life. Any time he comes here in the middle of the day, he goes down into the well. If you want my opinion, he either belongs to the tribe of jinnis or is crazy. He doesn't have any tolerance for summer heat. I've told him many times that it's not good to bathe in a well. Especially this well that we use for drinking—the animals too."

The sound of splashing awakens a temptation in me. I get up and walk to the well, putting my hands on the wall and bending over to look down. It takes a while for my eyes to get used to the darkness and then I see him. He is on his back floating on the water. He looks up, his eyes two shining spots in the darkness.

His hoarse voice flies up. "Come down, Behruz. Come and cool yourself off."

When I straighten up, I see a pile of cement blocks near the well. Fear and anxiety fill me as I think about picking one up. I turn toward the fields, trying to push these thoughts out of my head. Before doing anything I need to talk to him. I need to go down into the well, to look at him eye to eye and ask him. If he admits it, I'll take him under the water. I don't know if I have the physical strength or whether I will come up alive, but I will try to take him under—or him and me both. I start pulling off my clothes. It's as if I'm not in control of myself and a force is pushing me into the well. Grabbing the rope, I lean over the mouth of the well.

"What are you doing?" Musa calls. "Don't do it. Don't go down. This man . . ."

I hold the rope tight and brace both legs against the wall, hanging in the air for a moment. Beneath me, the water glistens darkly.

I don't care what Musa says or thinks. I just want to go down and face Kemal.

I move lower, first one leg and then the next, holding the rope while I let my body slide down. I've gone only a few feet when the rope starts to slip from my hands. I try to hold it tighter but my palms begin to burn and the wall runs past my eyes in a flash. My back hits the water and I go under. Frightened, I start to kick as hard as I can until I manage to get my head above water. Coughing and breathing hard, I try to hold on to the damp wall, but my hands slide off. From the other side of the well, Kemal laughs and splashes water at me.

Suddenly a sharp voice echoes in the well.

"Come up, Behruz. Come up! Are you crazy, going down the well?"

I look up and see Musa, a dark figure against the soft blue circle of the sky.

"Come up, Behruz," Musa calls again. "This man is crazy. He will . . ."

Amid Kemal's laughter and the splashing of water, I don't hear the rest of what Musa is saying. I let go of the wall and start to sink. In the cool water I feel light and free. I stay under for as long as I can hold my breath. The water pushes against my eyelids and I hear a muffled sound that seems to be coming from the depths of the earth. I want to stay under forever and be a part of the imprisoned water. At the same time I wish the water would push up to the top of the well and run uncontrolled through the fields like a mad, pre-historical flood, uprooting whatever is in its way—the village, Musa and his herds, Kemal, the dead lemon grove, everything—washing away everything and quenching this old land.

I bring my head out of the water and look up. The sky looks far away and I see hands moving. It's Musa, gesturing.

"Come up, Behruz. Come up right now."

I struggle to breathe in the damp, heavy air. Fearful, I start to kick to reach the other side of the well. Finally I grab the rope. My body feels like a stone and there is no strength in my arms. I hang on for a moment, trying to pull myself up, but have barely gotten above the water when I fall and go under. Struggling, I try to keep my head above water.

"What's the matter, Behruz?" Kemal says. "Calm down. Hey, calm down."

"What are you doing? Let him come up," Musa calls.

"I'm not doing anything," Kemal yells back.

Their shouts echo and when I look up, it seems that the circular mouth of the well is narrowing and the well is going to collapse over me.

Kemal moves closer. "Let me help you," he says. "Here, hold on." He hands me the rope.

I take the rope. After a moment I put my feet in the slimy hole where Kemal points and I manage to pull myself up a little. He puts his hands under me and pushes me out of the water. With my feet against the wall and my hands holding the rope, I hang there. I hear the steady stream of water dripping from me and don't dare look up or down. I put my forehead against the wet wall. The smell of dampness and stagnant water is overwhelming. The old man's voice comes down on my head, sharper than ever.

"Come up!"

Kemal tries to push me up. "Go, man. Move your foot. Put it higher." The water raining down from me echoes in the well. I hate myself, hate my clumsiness, my fear, my not knowing what to do. Carefully I take one foot off the wall and put it higher, then move one hand higher up the rope, grabbing it tight. Little by little, I manage to move up. When I reach the top of the well, a wave of heat hits my face. I grab Musa's outstretched hand and pull myself up, sit down on the wall of the well to catch my breath. The old man goes on talking.

"Have you lost your mind, going down the well? And following him? He's crazy."

My chest and thighs are covered with mud. The wetness quickly evaporates from my skin and I start to feel the sun on my shoulders. I get up, walk to the platform, and sit in the shade of the building. I'm looking at the mouth of the well when Kemal's head pops up. He stays there awhile, staring at me as if he were aware of the reason

I went down the well. Then he climbs out. Standing there naked, he pulls up the rope, takes a few bottles out of the bucket, and brings them to the shade near where I'm sitting.

"What happened to you, Behruz? Did you see jinnis in the well?" He laughs. "I thought you were braver than that."

I don't have any patience for him.

"It was great, wasn't it? So cool down there." He points to the bottles of homemade vodka that he had brought up from the well. "They are for you. I got them a few days ago and put them in the well. It's the best place to hide them. They stay cool there underwater, away from the eyes of busybodies. It's good stuff, much better than what we had last week. Just wait until you taste it. It's very difficult to find anything good these days and it's getting more dangerous, you know? But I have my ways." He laughs. "And if we are ever caught by the Komiteh guards, I hope you can stand the whipping!"

I stare at him, hating his playfulness. He turns to Musa, who has gone back to smoking his water pipe.

"Musa, can you go get the sack from the rack of my motorcycle? I brought something for all of us."

When Kemal turns around, I see dark reddish stripes angling down from his shoulders to his hips, obviously the marks of lashes. I wonder what he did and when and where he was whipped—was it by the religious militia in the middle of a square in Shiraz? I'm sure Musa must know about it and yet hasn't mentioned it.

Inside the sack that Musa brings are bread and cheese, some grapes, and a radio. Kemal turns on the radio. The harsh voice of the announcer pushes the quietness away. He is talking about the war and the new offensive against the Iraqis. "With the help of the Almighty," the announcer goes on with a defining voice, "our brave Bassigies have pushed back the Baathist infidels, killing thousands of them, and are heading west to capture Basra, and Allah willing we are not going to stop until we free Jerusalem."

"I brought the radio to leave it here, so you won't be lonely," Kemal says.

I don't pay any attention, but Musa seems very pleased. "Excellent, Kemal," he says. "Now I can listen to the Farsi BBC broadcasting again. I used to do that until four months ago. Something has gone wrong with my old radio and needs fixing. Maybe you can take it to the city on one your trips."

"No problem," Kemal says. "Maybe I can fix it myself. If not, I'll take it to my friend in the city. He has a radio shop there and sold me this Toshiba radio for a very good price."

I feel restless and disappointed with myself. I get up and walk to the well and lower the bucket down. My palms smart as I pull the rope up. I wash the mud off my body, put my clothes on, and walk to the Naranjestan. I want to be alone, to be away from all this confusion. The voices on the radio are sharp and sound unnatural and invading. The trees and a few lemons and oranges hanging from some of them are covered with dust blown in from the desert. I can sense their fragrance in the hot afternoon air and wonder how they can ever ripen without being irrigated. By this time of the summer the branches should start to be weighed down with fruit, but many of them are bare. The insistent sound of cicadas makes me feel dizzy. I stop to urinate and feel a sharp burning as each drop slowly drips out of me. I go to my usual spot under the willow tree and sit down facing the horizon. The sun looks like a huge copper tray and the golden color of the sky is joining the yellow of the desert and slowly turning to red.

Kemal calls me, but I don't want to move. He calls again. Musa calls too. After a while I get up and go to them. A tablecloth is spread out on the sitting platform, the same one, old and worn, that Musa brought from home. Kemal opens one of the bottles and fills two small cups. He puts one in front of me, says, "Be salaamati," and dumps the other one down his throat. He closes his eyes and pushes his lips together, tasting the liquid.

Musa shakes his head. "This is poison," he says. "No one should drink homemade arak."

"Homemade?" Kemal snaps back. "This is good stuff. Genuine. It's smuggled into the country from Iraqi Kurdistan—I have my sources." He turns to me.

"Let me tell you a story. I heard it the last time I was in Shiraz. You know that more and more Russians are coming into our country these days. Americans are out, Russians are in! Behruz, did you know I used to work with American engineers? I was a mechanic working in the refinery on the way to Shiraz. When the revolution came, they left and the project stopped. I lost my job. Well, these Russians, a group of them, seven of them, in a house in the holy city of Mashhad, where no one should be drinking"—he emphasizes these words—"drank homemade vodka made from figs and all went blind. Ha, ha, ha." He laughs loudly. "Imagine that. Seven Russians, blind and drunk, in the streets of the holy city of Mashhad."

"All the more reason you shouldn't drink this," Musa says.

Kemal, ignoring him, signals to me. "Drink, man! You won't go blind."

I don't want to drink but think if I have a few shots, I might get the courage to confront him. I empty the cup into my mouth and feel a sting in my throat. Tears come to my eyes and I start to cough.

Musa grumbles. "Don't, don't drink. Your insides are still bruised. It's worse than poison for you." Angrily, he turns to Kemal. "Are you planning to kill him?"

Kemal looks first at me, then at Musa. "I'm not holding a gun to his head, am I?"

"I'm afraid you may do that too," Musa says, staring at him with his one eye.

"Old man," Kemal says, "can you let us sit here in peace or are you going to start all your nonsense again?"

He winks at me and downs another shot. I chew a piece of bread to take away the burning in my mouth. "It's all about the war these days," he says, switching off the radio. After a while he gets up and goes inside the farmhouse, and we hear the sound of things being pushed and shoved around.

"He went to get his smoking things," Musa says. "He hides them in there."

Kemal comes back with a plastic sack and addresses Musa. "Go get the propane burner. I have something I know you're dying to have."

Musa leaves his water pipe beside the wall and gets up in a hurry as if he's been waiting for this order.

I wonder what he has to offer that Musa will be interested in, but I don't pay any attention and at the moment am dazzled by the glowing red and purple of the approaching sunset.

Musa comes back with a burner and lights it. It hisses and burns with a bluish flame. From the sack Kemal takes out a thin piece of wire about a foot long, a couple of plastic straws, and something small wrapped in a piece of paper. He places everything neatly in front of him on the tablecloth. Then he fills up the cups with vodka and, raising his, pours it down his throat in one motion and then makes a loud clicking sound with his tongue. He picks up the other cup and holds it out to me. I push his hand away.

"Behruz, tell me what's the matter. You don't want to drink with me? Have I done something wrong?" He puts the cup down in front of me and picks up a piece of cheese that he wraps in some bread and leaves beside my cup. "What is so bad about a little vodka that they've made it illegal to drink?"

He turns to Musa. "You tell me, old man. Did Muhammad the prophet ever say anything about bottled drinks? No, he just said don't drink, and he must have meant the drinks that were kept in jars or animal skins or whatever they used to have in those days. Certainly there were no bottles like this. If you ask me, he didn't say anything about bottled drinks! So why are these mullahs against it, then?" He laughs and turns to me. "Don't look at Musa sitting there smoking his pipe. He doesn't believe in anything. In his youth he did it all. I've heard how he used to go to the city and stay there for weeks."

Musa acts as if he hasn't heard a thing. "I'll be back in a minute," he says, getting up. "I need to check on the animals down by the Naranjestan."

When he's gone, I point to my eye and gesture to Kemal to tell me what has happened to Musa's eye.

"Well, man," he says, "why don't you ever say a word? What's the matter with you? What are you trying to prove?"

He pauses and then begins to explain. "His eye . . . I don't exactly know. I heard he was bitten by an insect after falling asleep in the desert. I've never asked him. But you know what I think? I think he got in trouble on one of his trips to the city a few years ago. I've heard many stories about him—about his father too."

Hearing Musa's footsteps, he stops talking and busies himself unwrapping the piece of paper. Inside is a chunk of opium that he places on a saucer and cuts into bits using a small knife. With one hand he holds the tip of the wire to the burner's flame and with the other picks up one of the plastic straws and puts it between his lips. When the wire glows red, he holds it on top of the opium, barely touching it. Then he bends closer, putting the end of the straw above the burning opium. The coil of silvery smoke has a smooth, enticing smell. It rushes into the straw as Kemal draws on it. He does all this so quickly and skillfully that not a bit of smoke gets away. The sequence is repeated until the little piece of opium is all gone. Then he drinks the sweet tea that Musa puts in front of him.

"I bet you've never seen anything like this, Behruz."

I shake my head.

"That's what I thought. They don't have this in America, do they?"

I shake my head again.

"Yes, this is called *sikh-o-sang*—wire and stone. It's becoming popular all around the country. It's more efficient than the old way, smoking with an opium pipe. We've modernized." He points to the propane burner and laughs. "Opium is very popular nowadays. It pours in from Afghanistan like water into the desert, and we Iranians are drinking it dry to the last drop."

Musa nods in agreement. I want to say, you're not telling me something I don't know, but stay quiet.

Kemal drinks his tea and winks at me. "Come closer, Behruz. It's your turn."

Temptation fills me, along with suspicion. I look at Musa, who has moved closer and has his eye on the opium. To my surprise, he doesn't object. He probably thinks that it will be good for me, that it will relax me. Kemal hands me the straw and holds the hot wire over the opium. As I suck on the straw, the smoke warms my throat and chest and I start to cough.

"Slow and smooth—don't rush it," say Musa and Kemal at the same time. I take a deep breath and suck on the straw again. I see Musa's excitement, as if he were participating in a ritual act. He hands me a cup of tea. "Drink," he says, "it will take away the bitterness."

"Here." Kemal hands Musa a small piece of opium. "You're killing me with that pathetic look of yours."

Musa gazes at the piece on the tip of his finger, his head cocked.

"What's this? A beggar would be disappointed too."

"Don't be so greedy, old man," says Kemal. "After you smoke this, you'll fall asleep for a week!" I notice as Kemal stretches out on the kilim that his runaway eyes have quieted down.

"Me, greedy? Not at all." Musa, shaking his head, holds the opium between his fingers. "This stuff is the friend of old age and the enemy of youth. It's good for a person like me. It takes the pain out of old bones. I'm not greedy—and let me tell you, nothing is greedier than opium itself and the opium pipe with its tiny hole."

I'm not paying any attention to them, captivated by the huge sun on the horizon.

"Listen to me," Musa says in a calm voice. "It's been said that the eye of an opium pipe can suck in a caravan of camels, fields of crops, entire buildings, and life, and youth. All can vanish right through its tiny opening as small as the eye of a needle." He stares at me. "Do you know what I'm talking about? Have you seen the opium pipe? Opium should be smoked with a pipe as in the old days, not like this."

He stops talking and draws on the straw. "Well . . . Do you know the origin of the opium plant? The plant we call *khashkhash*? The plant with its beautiful flowers, princess of all the flowers? Who knows when it all started. It was probably at the beginning of time." He closes his eye as if letting the smoke awaken the images in his mind. After a moment he begins to speak in a softened voice.

"*Yeki bood, yeki nabood*—once there was, once there was not . . . Yes . . . at this time of no time, there was a king who had a beautiful daughter called Khashkhash."

Ah, Khashkhash—so the opium poppy was named for a princess. I never know, though, whether the old man makes up stories based on the situation or just adds something to the folkloric stories he knows. I remember a few days ago his telling me about Zainolabedin, a man in the village who had an old book that he used to find the answers to people's questions about the future. Many people believed it didn't exist, although some said it had been in Zainolabedin's family for generations. Musa said he would love to have a book like that. Although I think he doesn't need any book to spark his imagination.

Musa takes in the smoke, holding his breath for what seems a long time, and then goes on with his story. "Yes, Khashkhash the princess was as beautiful as a flower. She was nearing the age of marriage when she gradually began to grow weak and pale. Doctors were called in from all over the regions under the king's rule. But none of them was able to discover the problem with the princess. Then one day out of nowhere, an old Chinese wise man, a man as old as China herself, walked into the palace. He had a long white beard and was wearing a yellow silk robe and carrying a beautifully carved walking stick. As soon as he saw the princess and looked into her eyes, he became excited and asked to talk to the king in private. He told the king that he had been searching for someone like the princess for years. He explained that through the centuries physicians had been looking for a person with the same symptoms as those of the princess. The king nervously watched the wise man, whose eyes shone with excitement. The Chinese wise man reassured the king, telling him not to worry, because the outcome of all this was going to be wonderful and would be useful to humanity for a long time to come. But there was a price to be paid.

"The king grew agitated. 'Whatever it is' he said, 'tell me, I'll pay. I'll do whatever will save my Khashkhash.' The wise man hesitated at first, and then explained to the king that someone must be sacrificed to cure the princess."

Musa pauses, looking at me and Kemal, then turns his face toward the fields as if trying to remember the rest of the story.

"Of course, kings are always good at things like this. They can sacrifice all the people if necessary. Well, the wise man told the king that if His Majesty wished the princess to be saved he must do exactly as he tells him without asking why. The king accepted. The wise man said first that the princess must be married to a young man who is a virgin. Second, that about nine months after the marriage the husband would die and must be buried in a sunny spot in the palace garden. Third, that the princess must pour water over his grave every day. And fourth, that the king shouldn't say a word about this to anyone.

"The Chinese wise man said he would be back when the time was right and left the same way that he had come, without anyone noticing where he went. As soon as he was gone, the king arranged for the princess to be married to the Governor of the East, a handsome young man whom the king did not trust. He was afraid the governor was waiting for a chance to revolt against him. But one thing the king didn't know was that the princess was in love with the Governor of the East and had met him secretly many times. Of course the princess happily accepted the marriage. There was a big wedding with all the marvelous things that happen when a princess marries. The newlyweds were very happy. They spent all their days in the palace gardens, strolling by the winding streams and making love under the willow trees. It was as if they were free of everything earthly and were living in heaven. The sound of their laughter and joy was heard all day long as if they were intoxicated by some mysterious essence. Day by day, the princess started to get better and the husband weaker, until he died exactly nine months to the day after the wedding. He was buried the way the Chinese man had described, and his grave was watered by the princess. No one ever heard her laugh again. Some say that the grave and the ruins of the palace are somewhere around here."

Musa looks at me and moves his hand in a half circle. "There is a place—maybe I'll take you there one of these days—where people have heard strange sounds, sounds of a woman, sometimes laughing, sometimes wailing. I think I have heard them myself. It was an unusually hot day and I was searching for one of my lambs that had gotten away. It was a dreadful sound. I got out of there fast. Even though I saw the hoofprints of the lamb, I didn't dare to go on looking for him."

He becomes quiet for a moment, cocking his head as if listening for something. I turn and look at Kemal. His eyes are closed and he's breathing calmly. I think he is pretending to be asleep.

"A month or so later there grew from the grave a clump of plants with long stems and beautiful flowers that no one had ever seen before."

Musa waits and I think he is surely lost in his own story, trying to picture the flowers blooming.

"As soon as the flowers appeared, the Chinese wise man came back out of nowhere. He watched the flowers every day, until their petals dropped and the only thing that remained was a seed case that looked like an egg topped with a crown. In the heat of the afternoon the wise man scored the seed cases with a razor and the next morning collected the milky sap that had oozed out and was turning brown. He repeated the same thing for several days and then one day picked the seed cases, which were full of hundreds of tiny gray seeds. Those were the seeds of the poppy flower, the source of this opium, you know."

Musa puts the tip of the hot wire on the opium and takes a couple of deep breaths.

"The day the wise man was leaving, he explained to the king that the extract from this rare plant could reduce pain and do miracles in the field of medicine, all thanks to his beautiful princess. But one thing the wise man failed to realize was the love that was in the princess's heart. That mysterious power added a dreadful complication to the outcome of his experiment." He points to the last fragment of opium in his hand. "Yes, love. Love caused this thing to have a duality—devastation or salvation. On the one hand it reduces pain, on the other it can devastate a person's life."

"Well, wise old man," Kemal says, half-asleep, "what can we do? The Chinese man and the king were not wise enough, and we have to suffer because of it."

"That's the way everyone talks these days," Musa grumbles. "It's always someone else's fault."

Kemal props himself up on one elbow and looks at me. "This drug problem is all over the place, isn't it, Behruz? In America you probably saw all sorts of drugs—like heroin. Is it true that if you take it, you think you can fly? Or you see a puddle of water and think it's a lake?"

I think about all the things I've heard about America since I've come back and wonder how people hear and repeat and make up things about a place they've never been to.

"Well, Behruz Khan?" It's the first time he's addressed me with the honorific Khan, and I can hear the sarcastic tone in his voice. Realizing I'm not interested in answering, he goes on. "It must have been nice in America. Why did you come back, man? How could you leave those blonde, blue-eyed women and come back?"

"Tell me, man. Why?" he asks again after a minute.

Slowly the feeling fills me that I'd like to get up and put my foot on his neck until he tells me everything he's been up to.

"They say America is very green, and its farms are all mechanized, that everything is done by machines. Is it true that in America there are farms so huge they could produce wheat and corn for the whole city of Shiraz?"

The vast plain of Nebraska with its yellow stalks of corn flies past my closed eyes.

"To tell you the truth," says Musa, "I can't figure out God's doings at all. He has offered too much water and greenery to one place and to another . . . well, look"—he points around us—"a land burning for a drop of water."

"The work of our God is beyond fairness, dear Musa," says Kemal. "He has not only provided beautiful nature to some places like America but also gifted them with many other things. Like the heavenly blonde angels. But to us, he has promised everything good in the next life. Isn't it true, Behruz?" He looks at me with sleepy eyes.

"Not everything is the act of God," Musa says. "It's in people's hands too. If people were hardworking and honest, if they weren't corrupt, they could change this desert into green. You tell me, Behruz, don't I tell the truth? I bet the people over there don't have the wickedness that people have here. Am I right?"

Kemal sits up and laughs. "Dear old man. You're probably right. But if I could hold hands with one of those blondes, I would be able to do much better too. I know that people there work hard and also that they enjoy life. I saw that when I worked with them at the refinery. Always at the end of the week they would go to an orchard on the side of the mountain not far away. They had friends who were professors at Pahlavi University and doctors at Namazi Hospital who came too. I went with my foreman, his name was Bill—can you believe that someone's name could be 'shovel'? He was a small man compared with all the other Americans. We called him Bill-che, Little Shovel. They would eat, drink, and have a good time. I learned some English too. Bill would talk to me with the little Persian he knew, 'Keemal, mard-e khobi'—good man. I forgot all the English I learned, though. I only remember 'Good morning. How are you? Very vell, tank you.'"

He looks at me and laughs.

"Well, there were a few women too," he goes on with excitement. "There was one who taught English at the university. She made me crazy when she lowered her blue eyes. Her name was Katy. She had short blonde hair and I liked looking at the back of her bare neck. She had big breasts"—he cups his hands against his chest—"this big. She was very quick in learning Persian and very different from her friends. She didn't drink or eat meat. It was strange to me. I thought they all drank. Sometimes she would spread out a blanket and sit for a long time meditating. Once I walked up to her slowly and put a flower between her fingers." He touches his thumb to his forefinger like a yogi. "She looked at me and smiled. Then I asked her, 'You, me, party?' and pointed behind the trees. She laughed and pinched me like this." He leans over and pinches Musa's cheek. Musa pushes his hand away.

"And she said, 'Keemal, tu divone-ie.'"

Musa laughed, "She was right about that. *Tu divone-ie.*"

"I told her to say it in English," Kemal went on, "and she said, 'You crazy.' Is it right, Behruz?"

I nod. He winks at me and then turns to Musa. "See—I know some English. I can learn very fast. Maybe Behruz will teach me."

When he's calm, his black eyes smile and there is a lightness in his movements, as if he were free of everything—free from any attachment, despair, or fear. He loves this life despite all its difficulties and all the problems that have turned up in society in the past few years. He doesn't just talk about his dreams but tries to follow the ones he thinks are achievable. Every time he comes here, he talks about this land, about reviving it. He wants to fix the pump and irrigate the orchard.

He's been trying in whatever way he can to convince me to let him start working the land. These days when everyone is running away from farming, he wants to farm. In my heart I believe him and am coming to doubt what Musa has told me about him.

Kemal smiles and asks, "Did you have a woman there? I know that those blue-eyed American girls love dark-eyed men like us.

Come on, Behruz, tell us. Why don't you talk? Why don't you ever say a word?"

"Leave him alone," Musa says.

The truth is, I don't have anything to share. I'm just enjoying hearing about the things that he had picked up working with the Americans. My mind starts to drift to Juanita, wondering how she is, when Kemal, agitated, says, "Well, you can't just not talk, especially if I'm going to be here. There's so much I'd like to know. About what it's really like in America and if the things we hear are true. And why the Iranian students over there, instead of enjoying themselves, being happy and studying, started demonstrating against the Shah? I used to hear all about it over the BBC radio. They must have been all these spoiled rich kids from big cities." He glances at me. "If people like me had been given the opportunity, I bet you things would have been different."

"What do you mean?" Musa asks.

"What I mean is, if I had had a chance to go to college, get a degree, I would have done much better. I would have learned more. Even with my lack of education, when I was working with the engineers, some of them foreigners, I could see that having a good job makes a world of difference. But look and see what we have now. Where are all those engineers? Gone with the industries shut down or bombed by the Iraqis. Why? Because a bunch of rich kids at the universities and the crowds who followed the mullahs were a bunch of useless people . . . The mullahs think praying is the answer to any problem. If it were, believe me, it would be as green as a jungle here with all the praying people do for rain . . ."

Not paying any attention, I lie down and stretch out, letting the vibrations of the cicadas take me away. Slowly my eyelids get heavier and Kemal's voice fades from my consciousness . . .

I'm in a crowd of students. Our faces are covered by paper masks with holes for our eyes. We walk in front of the student union shouting—first in Persian, then English, and finally in Spanish. "Down with the Shah!" "Carter stop supporting the Shah!" "Down with imperialism!" The police and a group of American students are standing around looking at us. Then we get on a bus for Washington, D.C., and sing labor songs and "The Internationale" . . . We reach Pennsylvania Avenue and see that it is full of police on horse-back. President Carter is welcoming the Shah to the United States. We're marching in front of the White House, students against the Shah on one side of the street and students supporting the Shah on the other. Suddenly people are rushing in all directions. We're hit-ting them, they're hitting us, and the police are grabbing anybody they get their hands on. The voice of President Carter is drowned out by the slogans and the wail of sirens. Clouds of smoke and tear-gas are carried toward the guests and journalists. The Shah wipes his eyes with his white handkerchief. Princess Farah tries not to show her tears . . .

"Where are you, Behruz?" I hear Kemal's voice. "Are you gone again? Gone to America? Forget it, my friend. Come back here with us. Come back to the desert. Why don't we work on this water pump and get it going? What do you say, Behruz?"

I realize he never talked this openly in front of Musa.

"Let's rebuild this place," he goes on. "Let's revive the Naranj-estan. Give it another chance. Give it water and make it green. What do you say, Behruz? How about it?"

Nine

MUSA, HAVING FINISHED SMOKING his share of the opium, is quiet, probably fallen into daydreams of his youth. The propane burner is off and Kemal has put away his smoking articles. He has stretched out and I hear his soft breathing. I can't recall how the day started but remember going down into the well and am amazed at myself for doing it. Now, lying here on this warm evening, a feeling of lightness floods my body cell by cell, a sensation like floating on top of calm water. My eyes are barely open and my ears are tuned to the silence around us.

"Tell us about America," Kemal says dreamily. "Did you like it there?"

"Let him sleep," Musa says.

"Sleep? He's always asleep! Tell us, Behruz. Tell us about the girls, about the women there."

I smile and think of Juanita with her straight black hair and round face and high cheekbones. I remember her lying naked on the bed in my apartment in the hot midwestern afternoon with me next to her and the ceremonial music of the crickets in the backyard. She laughs, then is quiet. We've just made love in the rickety old bed that pulls out of the wall. "You can sleep on this Murphy bed," my landlady said when she showed me the apartment. What a surprise it was when she pulled it down. I had never seen anything like it, and what nights I had on that bed with Juanita. Making mad passionate love all night in the old sagging bed that squeaked pleasantly and then falling asleep with our bodies entangled in the sheets. It was as if heaven had been brought down to earth in an old apartment building on a quiet street in a small midwestern town.

I remember how she would laugh and turn her back to me and how I would hold her tight and move my palm gently over her flat belly. "Listen," she would say, "lie still and listen to your mind." I would concentrate and listen, feeling as if I were stretched out on the bottom of a stream with water rushing over me.

Often on summer evenings we would drive to a prairie to watch the hundreds or even thousands of fireflies blinking like stars at eye level, going on/off, on/off just above the tallgrass. Once in a while a whistling train would pass in the distance or a church bell would ring from a nearby town. I would catch one of the fireflies in midair, holding it prisoner and feel the soft tickling on my palm. Then I would peep between my fingers to see it winking at me with a dim greenish light. Each time I was as astonished as the first. Juanita told me how she and her sister used to collect them in a glass jar and take them to bed to look at under the blankets.

"Talk, Behruz." I hear Kemal again. "Tell us about America—if you don't want to talk about the girls there, tell us about the cities—the great cities—and the people."

"Let him rest," Musa says. "Let him be."

The great cities . . . I think of New York City. How could I describe New York or Chicago, with their skyscrapers and crowded streets, or any American city for that matter? One has to see it, walk it, hear it, and smell it in the morning, at midday, in the afternoon, in the evening, or late at night. I think of the cafés and streets of New York, a city full of impatient people hurrying around, walking, jogging, and bicycling. A city where every language of the world can be heard:

"Hey man—watch it, man!"

"¿Qué pasa, mi amor?"

"As-salamu alaykum."

"Hia, hia. Chotto matte."

"Che tori? Che khabar?"

A city of all kinds of sounds, and at every corner tall buildings of steel and glass stretching upward like giant arms praying to God. And everywhere music—in the streets, in the stores, in the elevators, coming up out of the basements. A city that throbs continuously, as if holding the heart of the world in her chest. That vibrates constantly from subways, like fast-flashing worms moving in her belly.

How could I describe America? The America I found was a land of ideas and a can-do attitude. It was where a self-made people put down the first brick not long ago and have built a nation unique in many ways. History seemed always to lay lightly there, the scars of the past never dimming hope and optimism toward the future. Iran by contrast seemed an old nation not able to break with its past, a past that is a heavy load not just dragged behind but also controlling the future. Even its last drastic push for freedom, bought with the blood of its most able young generation, is lost in the desert of centuries-old belief. It's as if the train of time had left us many stations back while we were busy with our past and our God.

How could I explain America? America of the Fourth of July and hot dogs. A country open to all nationalities and any religion, with temples, mosques, synagogues, and churches standing next to one other. A country of tree lovers, animal lovers, bird lovers, Jesus lovers, drug lovers, music lovers, sports lovers, gun lovers, peace lovers . . . And which America should I describe? A country of people who won't hurt a dog or a cat but are able to wage wars on people thousands of miles away? A nation proud of having saved Europe from the Fascists or one still wounded and confused about Vietnam? A place where hardworking people proudly say, "It's a free country," or where you hear constantly, "There is no free lunch."

I went everywhere in America with no problem, except for once in Kansas when we stopped at a place selling used furniture and an old black man in a rocking chair asked me where I was from.

"Iran," I answered.

"Eye-ran?" he said in a low voice, almost a whisper. I had to lean down to hear him. "Didn't you people have our hostages?"

I stood still—it was the first time in all my years in America I had been confronted like this.

"Hush, Daddy," a young man told him, coming over to shake hands with me.

"Sorry, man," he said. "Don't mind him—he's just old."

Once we drove west across Iowa and Nebraska toward the open horizon, going through a sea of pastures and fields of yellow-tasseled corn. As we crossed the Sandhills, Juanita told me about her Indian ancestors. She talked about the way white America romanticizes the Native Americans to give itself a past and how nostalgia for the past runs straight through Native American history. How even the peace and environmental movements draw spiritual guidance from Native Americans—the love of nature and the idea of living in harmony with the natural world all having their roots in Native American culture.

Her laughter is still in my head and I can hear her telling me that they even gave America its Hollywood. "Without Indians," she said, "there would be no Westerns. No John Wayne or Clint Eastwood." I knew these actors from the movies that poured into Iran when I was growing up and gave my generation the idea that all of America was the Wild West.

We stopped by a field and walked to a stream. She was talking, and for a moment my mind drifted to the dry fields of the Naranjestan. Then her touch brought me back to the green fields in front of us, a place where her ancestors in the long-gone days used to set up their villages and hunt buffalo. She squeezed my hand, her gaze fixed on the horizon—I can still see her standing there on the hill where the sky was the only border. She talked of her ancestors' way of life, of their wars and the blood that was spilled so they could stay faithful to the land. She told me about the Ghost Dance and the massacres at Wounded Knee and how she wanted to take me to South Dakota, to the place where Big Foot fought and was killed beside a frozen stream. She described the scene as if she were witnessing it. On one side of the stream are blue-uniformed soldiers, on the other side women, children, and old people. Everyone is confused, running in different directions. The guns thunder and the frightened horses neigh, their breath steaming out into the cold air. There is Big Foot frozen in the snow, half standing, even in death looking like he is rising to fight.

"Hey, Behruz," I hear Kemal say. "Wake up, man. The stars are out and the moon is early tonight."

Then I hear Musa's old voice. "Well, the day is gone and I'd better go to see if my herds found their way home."

Opening my eyes I see the flickering stars above and listen to Musa reciting a poem by Hafez as he gathers himself up to leave.

> Heaven's fields are green and the moon's a sickle
> it's time to harvest not to sow
> yes the sun is high and lady luck fickle
> but life unfolds and disappointments go.

Ten

"H E'S GONE AGAIN—he's gone back to America again."
My eyes barely open, I see two people, shadowlike and close by. They move around whispering and then shuffle away.

. . . I'm in a canoe in the middle of an icy lake. I'm shivering from cold. The day is gray and it is hard to know if it's morning or afternoon. Land, trees, and fog merge in the distance. There are three men in the canoe with me. All are wearing long black coats with hoods. Their eyes glow like dim neon lights when they look in my direction. We're searching the water. Something dangerous is around us or something bad is about to happen and we are here to prevent it. The silence is deep and there is a tension in the air as if we were surrounded by a magnetic field. We seem to be in this place to find something we can't see, hear, or smell.

The man who appears to be in charge takes something out of his pocket. It looks like a book with a black-leather cover. With a swing of his arm he throws the object ahead of us. It travels in the air for a short distance and then skips on the slippery surface of the ice. For a moment I see it, a dark shadow in the greenish water, sinking slowly. He points toward it, and we quickly paddle to the spot. The sound of the oars hitting the water and floating ice breaks the silence. The same man plunges his hand into the water and brings up the object. He shakes it off and holds out his arm. For the first time I see his face. There is something odd about him—he is bent over and has a tiny head with an unusually long neck that rises from the middle of his shoulder at an angle. It looks like he has a beak instead of a mouth. With the object still in his hand, he points east and then west, making a semicircle, then puts the thing back in his pocket. I understand that he has pointed out an uncrossable boundary.

. . . The large room is full of people, some sitting and some lined up against the walls. No one knows what we're waiting for and everyone seems to be confused. The heat is unbearable and we keep wiping our faces. A few men come and go, bringing files or taking them away. The place appears to be some kind of judicial office. There are shelves full of files and stacks of papers piled up against the walls. A man sitting behind a desk is facing me. Once in a while he looks up from a folder in front of him and stares at me with sharp eyes. Unlike the rest of us, who are breathing uneasily because of the heat in the room, he appears to be cold and is wearing a heavy coat. He opens a file and asks me, "Do you recognize this handwriting?"

I do—it looks like the handwriting of a woman I know. Then he opens another file. "How about this one?" he says impatiently. I realize it is the same person's handwriting, although looking somewhat different. I think it is either Alexandria trying to imitate Cynthia's handwriting or Cynthia trying to imitate Alexandria's handwriting. I know both women, but when I try to remember my relationship to them, my mind doesn't cooperate.

The man shouts at me over the noise in the room, "I see from your reaction that you know the handwriting." Then he snaps the file shut.

I can't understand if there is a complaint against me or if it's all a setup.

He opens an old book, worn out by use and with smudge marks on the pages. "Look through this," he says. "You're free to choose the punishment you will receive."

I look at the first pages and then the next and the next. They are all the same, written in archaic glyphs I don't recognize. Each line on each page is exactly the same. I start to say I don't understand, but he looks at me in silence. For the first time I see that both sides of his head are flat and he has no ears.

"Enough," the man says. "It doesn't matter. We know the punishment for your type. It is always the same—from ancient times the same."

. . . The sky and the trees in fall colors ripple on the river's surface beneath a soft drizzle. I stop walking to look around. I must be in a foreign land, but someplace I have been before. It seems so unusually peaceful that it makes me nervous. I walk quickly into the woods. Dry leaves crumble under my feet. Soft rain falls on my head as I keep walking and searching. What I'm searching for and what direction I'm going in, I don't seem to know. Amid the dense shadows of the forest, I see movements. A nude woman appears from behind a tree and disappears behind another. Then I see another woman and yet another. There are as many women as there are trees. They move as if they are aware of me. I follow them until through the trees I see a shimmering surface, the edge of a pond. On the far side of the water flocks of ducks are swimming. I stand still and don't hear anything except the drip, drip of the rain all around me. I watch ducks dive under the water, one after another, bobbing . . . up and down, up and down.

I watch in silence, how long I don't know. Suddenly I am startled by a man who comes up behind me. He is wearing a bright-orange outfit, carrying a rifle.

"What are you doing standing here?" he says. "Don't you know you should be wearing orange in the woods?"

There is something about him that makes me shiver. It's not his gun or his shouting. It's his face. His eyes are two empty holes and his smile is a smile and a frown at the same time. I take a step back and at the moment that I turn and face the pond, the ducks take flight flapping above me, and when I look at the water, the circles of ripples move toward the edge of the pond and die by my feet.

Eleven

I 've been watching for Musa all afternoon, hoping to see
him on the road from the city. Early this morning I gave him
the key to the house in Shiraz and asked him to go and find the old
leather briefcase that belonged to my father. All the important family papers are in that briefcase, plus a little sum of money. I hoped
the briefcase would still be there. Musa agreed to go without even
asking what was in the briefcase. "I owe more than that to your family" was the only thing he said.

He should have been back by early afternoon. From the village it's
only an hour by foot to the city road and from there another half-
hour or so to Shiraz by bus or car.

Now I'm afraid it wasn't safe to send him. I'm not sure why I
asked him or why he agreed. Just because Father did something for
him or his family? Musa has brought this up a few times without
revealing anything. What sort of obligation could it be that he, such
a cautious man, would put himself in danger? Then I think maybe
he's late because he decided to go to the market before coming back.

I wish Kemal would come. He hasn't been around for a few days.

He promised he would help with anything I need, but where is he now? I could have sent him to the city or had him go with Musa. I should have realized that the house could be a trap—that maybe it's being watched, if it hasn't been confiscated by now. But Musa is a wise man, a careful man. He would know not to go in if there were any danger.

At noon I drew water from the well for Musa's animals. They come back from the fields on their own. It's their routine. Maybe they can smell the water in the well. It wasn't easy to pull up the bucket with all of them around my legs pushing and shoving. I was afraid they would push me over the wall and down the well. As soon as I pulled the bucket up, dripping with water, they all rushed for it and I couldn't keep them away. They thrust their heads in, tipping the bucket over before I could empty it into the small round cement trough. I pulled them by their wool and didn't know they could be so stubborn. I tried to talk to them like Musa. "Hey, watch it," I shouted. "Wait, you'll get your chance." But it was no use. I had to draw up the bucket several more times, holding it up and pouring it into the trough from above their heads. My palms are still burning from pulling the rope.

I don't know what time it is but soon it will be getting dark. From my place under the tree, I can barely see the village in the afternoon haze. Today there were more people than usual on the village road. I counted five groups going to the city and three coming back. Once I thought I heard a woman wailing and wondered whether they were bringing back a war casualty.

This morning two figures came across the field and went toward the far end of the Naranjestan. I had seen them before, but usually very late in the afternoon. They seem to avoid coming to the well and farmhouse. No doubt they have seen me here. They always go into the far reaches of the Naranjestan and disappear there. Musa tells me about all sorts of people running around these days. Opium addicts, drug dealers, gun smugglers, thieves, and people who have nothing to do but wander around to pass the time. Some could be refugees from the war zones. But these two men always walk side by side, holding hands—something you see often in Iran, unlike in America. I have decided that they're harmless.

I'm sure that I told Musa the exact hiding place—inside the storage space under the staircase to the second floor. But under which step did I tell him? Did I tell him the tenth one? That's where Father had made a hiding place for the briefcase. All Musa had to do was push the board, put his hand under the stair, and take the briefcase.

Someone is coming. I can see that it is Musa from the way he walks leaning to one side. He isn't carrying anything. I wave to him anxiously. When he gets closer, I get up and walk toward him. He looks exhausted and anxious and doesn't look at me directly. His back seems more bent than usual. He draws water, then drinks and washes up. When we go over to the sitting deck, he takes a pack of cigarettes from his pocket and lights one. He must have bought them in the city. Talk, man, what happened? I want to say, but keep quiet. He sees the impatience in my eyes. "Let me catch my breath," he says, rubbing his nose. Then he takes off his hat and scratches his head, facing me with an excruciating look.

"It was terrible," he says in a dry, low voice. "Terrible. What a day. First of all, here is the key to the house. I couldn't find the briefcase. The house was in shambles. Things were scattered all over the place. It was obvious that it had been searched. I looked where you told me, under the staircase. It was dark and hard to see. I pushed all the boards, but none of them moved. I couldn't see inside. I thought I heard something like a door opening, then I realized it came from outside, from the yard. When I went out, I saw one of the neighbors watching from the second-floor window. An old man. When he saw me, he got his wife and they stood at the window and stared."

He puffs on his cigarette hurriedly, his hands shaking. I've never seen him so nervous.

"What a day to go to the city," he goes on. "It was my bad luck, I guess. In the square, the one close to your house . . ."

He looks at me with his one eye, talking fast and not giving me time to speculate. "There I was in the crowd of people gathered in the square. I didn't know why I stood there listening to people talking. Someone said they were going to punish a thief by cutting off his hand. Like the rest of them, I was waiting to see what would happen. Everyone was impatient, as if they wanted it to be finished so they could get on with what they'd been doing. One man—a boy, really—was talking about how he had seen a hand cut off. He talked as if he had done it himself. How the sweat was running down the face of the victim, who breathed hard and kept moving his fingers and touching them, not believing they would be cut off in a few minutes. How they brought the table out and put the victim's hand on it through the leather strap . . . He talked wildly. I thought he just was telling a story to amuse the people around him. I just stood there in the middle of the square in the hot sun listening to—to this boy. Then I heard someone say they're not going to cut off a thief's hand, they're going to hang someone."

He stopped for a moment. "Yes, it was a hanging day. They were going to hang two men, and I was there to see it. All sorts of people were there, even children with their parents. I'm glad I'm an old man and don't have much time to carry such awful images with me. I don't know what we have come to. Maybe it's a sign of the end of the world. I heard people say that the men were being punished for having affairs with married women. I also heard that they were drug dealers. Whatever. Do they think that by hanging criminals in public in the middle of the day, crime will stop? It was like the Devil himself had tied me to the ground to see what we humans are capable of. There were two big cranes in the middle of the square. They brought the two men out of a car, their heads covered with black sacks and their hands tied behind them."

I'm getting angry and upset and don't want to hear more, but the old man keeps talking. I think to myself, let him get it off his chest—it's my fault, after all, for sending him to the city.

"Everything happened very quickly. People became silent as soon as they saw the prisoners. The guards put the crane's cables around the prisoners' necks. Then I heard the crane engines roar, and suddenly these two poor men were hanging high in the air."

I feel my stomach turn and I get up. Musa gets up as well.

"It was like a nightmare," he goes on, "or like being awakened from a nightmare. I left the square quickly. My old legs dragged me away in such a hurry it surprised me."

Musa takes a few steps to leave. "It is not that I'm afraid of death," he stops and says. "Not at all. But a death like that I'm afraid of. It's the city and the people who go to watch this sort of dying that

I'm afraid of. I've seen many deaths in my life—natural deaths, you know. Natural death in a way is bearable. It's part of life. Life and death are inseparable twins. Natural death is peaceful. It's like going to sleep. The eyes close softly, the Adam's apple moves up and down a few times, and then nothing—the person falls into a sleep that has no awakening. But unnatural death is frightening because life doesn't want to go away and fights death with all its might. Watching that sort of death is painful."

He walks away a few steps and then stops. "I've got to go. I've got to go and find my herds. Sometimes I wish I could just live with them."

He hesitates for a moment and then continues. "I'm not sure, but I think I saw Ruzbeh."

"What? Where was this?" I ask, excitedly.

"I don't know if it was him. I couldn't see very well in the dark alley that goes to the house. I saw someone hurry up the alley and turn into the street. I thought it was Ruzbeh and went after him. I thought I saw him talking to someone on a motorcycle. I can't say it was Kemal. When the motorcycle drove away, he disappeared in the crowd. I tried to follow him. He went toward the square, but I couldn't go there again. It was like my legs wouldn't take me there. I went back to the house. It was dark inside, and I looked around to see if Ruzbeh had been there. I couldn't say. Things were scattered all over the place."

I feel so angry at myself that I am ready to punch my fist through a wall. I know if I had gone myself, I could have followed Ruzbeh and caught up with him.

"I'm sorry," Musa says. "I just couldn't find him. Maybe it was him, maybe not. I'll go back in a few days and look again, I promise. I need to go back to the city to see someone I haven't seen for years. I wanted to see him today, but it just didn't work out. Now I've got to find my animals before they get lost in the desert or wild dogs tear them apart."

I watch as he walks away, his figure fading in the evening dusk. I stand there not wanting to move, not knowing how to deal with my anger and hatred, certain only that it's going to be another long night.

Twelve

O ANCIENT CITY, I MURMUR as we pass under the Koran Gate, keep me safe and lead me on. Beloved city of poetry, roses, and nightingales, city of Hafez and Saadi, surviving the centuries in this valley squeezed between ragged mountains, standing in witness to times of love and peace, war and destruction. Your beauty saved you from the wildest of men. Even the Mongols bowed low, learned your language and your music, and were dazzled by your gardens and the magic of your poets. But what can save you from the wars of modern man and the enemies within and without, the ones who want love to die? Can they be fought with poems and roses?

Beloved city, keep me safe and keep Shireen and Ruzbeh safe if they are here within your walls. And shield me from those who are the enemies of love.

We speed past the Hafezieh with it's domed tomb surrounded by tall cypress trees, and I wish I could tell Kemal to stop the motorcycle so I can get off and walk in the garden and visit the resting place of the poet, but I have to do what I came here for. The city park with its old maple trees reminds me of my high school days when I used to hang out there with friends. Downtown Shiraz is bustling with people, traffic, and exhaust. As we travel toward the house, the city becomes greener and the air more fragrant. The tall trees of the famous Bagh-e Eram become visible behind the garden wall.

I didn't want Kemal to come with me to the house. In case of any problems, I think it would be better if he's not there. He leaves me some distance away, wishes me luck, and says he'll come by and wait for me at the entrance of the alley to the house.

Keeping my head down, I walk toward the house. My legs are rattling from the ride and I am still dizzy from the roar of the motorcycle and smell of its exhaust. I must hurry. The sun is setting and evening is on the way. I walk fast and try not to attract attention. The darker it gets the safer it is, but only before the night patrols come onto the streets. The words of the Koran are being broadcast from a minaret. A group of people with black-and-green banners stand in front of the mosque. Guards and mullahs, some in black turbans and some in white, are gathered by the door. I rush past them, trying not to think about the day I saw a similar group in the square, waiting for the stones to be cast.

The walls along the street leading to the house are painted with revolutionary pictures and slogans—"Down with America," "Islam is our way, Khomeini is our guide." Farther on there is a portrait of Khomeini looking at me out of the corner of his eye. Nothing escapes his notice. At the bakery, a group of women in black chadors are standing with their children, waiting to buy bread. I realize how hungry I am and how long it's been since I've had any freshly baked bread. When I get to the corner with the news kiosk, I think of stopping. The owner knows me and I see him inside. He's reading and a cigarette is dangling from his lips. I wish I could ask him if he's seen Ruzbeh or Shireen, but decide I can't risk it. Glancing at him I walk past quickly.

People are standing in line at the butcher shop and the grocery store, trying to finish their shopping and hurry home before the blackout starts. A few guards are patrolling the streets. There are piles of garbage here and there along the sidewalk and the sharp smell of car exhaust. A mass of dust and paper rises up and showers down with every vehicle that goes by. I walk past a street dog, skinny and nervous, searching through the trash.

It's getting darker and people are moving like shadows under the dim streetlights. Soon all the lights will be off, out of fear of the nightly MiG raids. Suddenly my shirt is pulled from behind and I have the impulse to run. I turn to see a beggar who mumbles, *"Komak, mahze khoda komak. Noon nadarm"*—Help, for God's sake, help, I've no bread. Having nothing to give him, I pull myself free and walk away at a faster pace.

A block or so before the alley, a band of boys, belts in hand, are noisily engaged—it's hard to say if they are playing or fighting. A couple of them are trying to hold down a boy who is struggling to get away. One is snapping a belt in the air and yelling, "Keep him down." I wonder if they are imitating a scene from the public floggings in the city square. They stop and stare at me, and for a moment I debate with myself whether they are planning to attack me or intimidate me. I rush by, remembering the days when I walked with my high school friends through these same streets without ever seeing such a thing. Our excitement was spending time in bookstores or at the movies. Who knows where my friends are now, especially those who were Jewish or Baha'is. I suppose that they are gone—vanished one way or another. Some I know are out of the country, but others may have been killed in the uprisings or are probably in jail.

I can't get caught up in the past. I need to concentrate on getting to the house and finding the briefcase without letting other things cloud my mind. In the alley, I slow down and look around. The alley is empty. At the door I manage to push the key in but can't help thinking of the night Shireen stood here with the zealots shouting at her and I was on the other side of the door, not having the courage to open it. I quickly turn the key, step into the courtyard, and close the door behind me, wondering if anyone saw me or if anyone is inside the house. I don't care anymore if they are waiting for me. The lemon and orange trees along the path to the house make it darker at this time of the day. At the front door, I don't hesitate, go in, and wait in the dark. I listen for any sound before turning on the flashlight that Kemal gave me.

"Ruzbeh? Ruzbeh, are you here? It is me—Behruz."

Nothing. My God, what has happened here? The house is empty and the beam of my flashlight hits piles of what is left here and there. The carpets and the furniture are gone. And my books and tapes have been thrown on the floor.

"Ruzbeh, are you here?" I call softly, going from room to room, but I don't hear anything.

The space under the staircase smells of dampness. The staircase zigzags in front of me and at the moment I raise my hand to push the board in, the thought hits me that the briefcase is not there. Either the people who have rampaged the place have stolen it like the rest of the household or Mother has taken it with her. I don't know why I didn't think about this in advance. I should have gone to Mother and asked her.

I push the board hard and it falls back with a dry cracking sound. Holding my breath and standing on my toes, I reach inside. My fingers touch the briefcase and I grab it and pull it out quickly. The soft dust scatters and makes me sneeze violently. I realize that Musa couldn't reach this high. He must have been looking under the step below. Then again, maybe I didn't explain very well.

Happy that I've found the briefcase but wondering why Mother hadn't taken it, I continue to look around and see that the first step in confiscating the house has occurred. Everything valuable has been taken. The final step would be some government person moving in. I wonder whether they would ever think of the people who once walked this hallway or were born or died here. Would they be fond of gardening and have a row of jasmine pots by the entrance the way Mother used to?

I look around for a few more minutes on the first floor. I don't want to go upstairs. The idea of going into Shireen's bedroom upsets me, but what if Ruzbeh is there? I walk up the old stairs, whose creaking breaks the silence. There's no evidence that Ruzbeh is here. I search the room and look in the closet. I wish I could find some sign of Shireen. I would like to find a dress of hers and wrap it around me, hide my face in it, but all the clothes are gone, all her jewelry is gone too. I try to smell the perfume she used to wear, but there is nothing, only the smell of damp air. The bed is pushed to the middle of the room with the mattress pulled halfway off. I push it back and long to see Shireen lying there, stretched out with her head resting on her arm, gazing at me as I walk back and forth and tell her about America.

I stand there looking at the bed when suddenly I hear something in the yard and run downstairs to the front door, thinking someone is coming in. No one is there, but there is something. I can hear something in the house, some strange noise coming from inside. I run through the yard and down the alley and out onto the street, hoping to find Kemal where he said he would be waiting. It's dark and the street is deserted. I find Kemal standing there by his motorcycle and run toward him, panting. He starts the motorcycle and I jump on behind, clasping the briefcase to my chest, unable to get rid of the thought that Ruzbeh was in the house.

Thirteen

I N THE PAST TWO DAYS my sickness has returned—the same
fever and chills that leave me feeling numb. What little progress
I've made in the past few weeks seems to be lost. It all began after
the trip to the city. I started to feel hot and then in a few minutes
was shivering as if I'd been thrown into ice water.

Musa has been staying late the past few nights and giving me all
sorts of boiled herbal medicines. He believes that *golgav zaban,* a
purple flower boiled with rock sugar, is good for a fever because it
has been used to cure the sick since the old days.

Last night under the dim kerosene lamp—it must have been at
the height of my fever—I opened the old leather case. I had been
avoiding doing this, thinking that I might find family secrets that
would cause me anxiety.

Everything inside was in disarray and had an old, dusty smell.
All I needed the briefcase for was for the deed to the Naranjestan.
I searched for it among the papers and envelopes and eventually
started to organize everything. I was distracted by the old black-
and-white photographs, looking at them and setting them aside.

Some were taken in the gardens of the house in Shiraz, some here in the Naranjestan. And then there were the ones I sent from America—pictures of Juanita when we were traveling together. I was surprised to find letters I wrote to Shireen when I was in the United States. Some dated from the first few weeks after I arrived and were full of emotion and nostalgia. Also the letters that I wrote asking Shireen and Ruzbeh to come to the United States were there, plus the ones where I had described my political activities with the international students in response to Shireen's letter about the student uprising in Shiraz and the women's activities she was involved in prior to the revolution. Later I wrote of my concern for Ruzbeh after his injury and to respond to Shireen's request that I come back to Iran for his sake.

While I was reading and daydreaming, I heard noises outside. Someone was walking around. Then I heard whispering. Panicked, I shoved everything inside the briefcase and blew out the lamp. I was sure that someone had seen me in the city and followed me here. Then it occurred to me that Kemal and Musa could be up to something, maybe thinking that I had money in the briefcase. I ran out the back door and hid among the trees, watching the house for I don't know how long. I dozed off a few times, but not seeing anything came back nervously. I couldn't sleep the rest of the night and early in the morning searched the soft dirt around the building. It's impossible, I thought. There must be footprints. Someone had been here in the middle of the night—I was sure of it. But I found no footprints. Could it be I imagined it at the height of my fever? Or was it just the wind? I went back inside, feeling feverish and tired, and lay down.

Now I feel a little better and sitting at my usual spot by the dry stream waiting for Kemal and Musa. Kemal hasn't been around since we went to the city and Musa should be bringing his herds for an afternoon watering. I have the open briefcase beside me and plan to organize everything, the pictures and letters and documents, putting them in piles and tying them up. I found the deed to the Naranjestan among the papers and put it aside. Among the other documents were the deed to the house in the city and the one in the village, the birth and death certificates—even my grandparents' and great-grandparents', and the marriage certificates—my parents' yellowing and brittle and Shireen and Ruzbeh's on clean white parchment. Ruzbeh's and Shireen's high school diplomas—I couldn't find mine, if I had taken it to America with me I'm sure I lost it there— and their university transcripts were there as well, plus their passports with expired U.S. visas. There was a surprise too—the birth and death certificates of my sister, a girl named Parvaneh, who lived for only a few months and died before Ruzbeh and I were born. I thought of her name, Parvaneh, which means butterfly. Mother had never mentioned her. Neither had Father. I thought of how Mother used to say Shireen was like her own daughter, when she was small and played with us in the Naranjestan.

I hear Musa calling from the platform and realize I must have dozed off. Kemal is standing beside him. I didn't hear or see them coming. Smoke is rising from the fire. Musa is probably preparing his water pipe and some herbal tea for me. I carefully gather all the papers and pictures and put them back in the briefcase, wondering if Kemal and Musa have seen them.

Before joining them, I walk to the Naranjestan, looking at the trees. There are many lemons scattered under them. They wouldn't have lost so much of their fruit if they had been irrigated in the spring and summer. I can't imagine where they get the moisture they need and how some have managed to bear a few fruits. They are covered with dust and rough to the touch. I wonder if the trees are aware of the desert extending toward them.

As I walk back to the house I see Kemal and Musa watching me. I suppose that I look odd carrying the briefcase. They're probably wondering what's in it that I've risked going to the city for and why I am carrying it around. I go and sit on the platform, wanting a cup of tea before I talk to them or show them the documents and tell them what I've done.

Musa has everything ready. He puts a cup of tea in front of me, the sweet steam rising, and urges me to drink. I pick up the cup, drinking slowly, and watch the fields and the Naranjestan. Things seem unusually quiet. The only sound is the bubbling of Musa's water pipe. There's no wind, and from here the trees look calm, as if they are resting. Musa fills up my cup again. Kemal says nothing. He seems agitated, and I wonder what they were talking about before I got here.

I open the briefcase, take out the deed to the Naranjestan, and hand it to Kemal. He looks at me and then at the paper. He realizes what it is and starts to read it through. I take a sip of tea, keeping the sweet, warm liquid in my mouth before swallowing. I see that Musa is uneasy. He glances at Kemal, who continues reading.

I can sense that Kemal doesn't believe what he is reading. He looks at me without a word and then turns his eyes back to the deed. At the bottom of the deed I have written a note signing my share of the property over to him and Musa. Kemal hands the paper to Musa without looking at me. As Musa slowly reads, I see the wrinkles twitching in his face. He looks at me, then at Kemal.

I have added at the bottom of the deed that Musa is a partner, that Kemal must pay the expenses of my mother and Shireen's mother while they are alive, and that if Shireen or Ruzbeh ever come back, they have to be taken care of as well. As for me, I've given myself no rights to anything—not the lemon grove, the water, or the land.

I wish I could know their thoughts, but both are silent. Then Kemal gets up and walks out to the Naranjestan. I watch him walking among the trees as if he were giving them the news. Musa doesn't move. He takes his handkerchief out of his pocket and wipes his bad eye. It's obvious he doesn't approve. He doesn't know that what I've done is not for him or Kemal or my sick mother or my wandering brother. Not even for myself. It is for the Naranjestan. I can't see it so thirsty any longer. I did it for the trees and the fields—for the trees I hate to see so barren and for the fields I can't bear to see so scorched. I did it for the water. The water that I don't want to be imprisoned in the well any longer but running free over this land, turning it green as in my childhood memories.

I think this is the best, maybe the only, thing I'm capable of doing at this time. The property is mine and Ruzbeh's, but I can't understand why it should belong to me, who has worked on it not even an hour. Should it be mine just because I was born into the family that owned it for generations?

I sit for a while and then get up and go to the Naranjestan, where a soft wind is singing through the lemon trees, and think of the days when we wondered whether there were jinnis living in the orchard and wished they would appear to grant our wishes.

Fourteen

I've lost count of the coming and going of the days, so slow in passing, and the nights, host to darkness and anxieties. My health gets worse each day. I'm either burning with fever or shivering with chills. It is as if my body and mind are being prepared for their end.

The weather too has undergone a metamorphosis. The air has picked up the sharp coldness of fall. Unlike the summer wind that loved to linger and sweep up to the dome of the sky whatever was in its path, the autumn wind blows constantly and is in a hurry. It howls and moves low to the ground with no particular direction, like an escaped prisoner running away from everything and everyone, not knowing where to go. I feel its chill constantly, no matter how long I lie in the sun or sit near the fire that Musa makes. My lungs won't accept the cold air and push it out quickly, feeling like they are going to collapse at any moment.

In the afternoon sun, the distant village is one with the bare fields beyond. A lone dog is barking and a sad voice carries with the wind. Maybe it's the cry of a mother mourning her lost child. Or the moaning of someone wandering aimlessly in the desert. I look toward the village road and search for the shapes of a woman and two children—Kemal's family. They've been coming to the Naranjestan since the day I handed over the deed. His wife brings food and prepares tea for us and has cleaned up the house and washed the old blankets and pillows. She's a young woman with a round face and, unlike the city women, dresses in bright-colored clothes. After lunch she draws water from the well and washes the dishes and makes tea before going back to the village. Sometimes the children stay all day and Kemal takes them home on his motorcycle. Musa's wife never comes here—he says she is old and has bad knees. The children play in the Naranjestan without coming near me. Their mother keeps her distance too. The boy, Amir, is six years old, with a sharp curiosity in his eyes. The little girl, Golboo, is four years old and has long black hair and the look of a sleepy cat. A few times I have thought about walking to the village, to see it up close, walk its narrow alleys, visit the school, and see where Musa and Kemal live. And if I can gather up my courage, possibly visit Mother.

The huge iron door of the pump house has been pushed open. It extends the entire length of the side of the building facing the orchard. Kemal is standing by the motor. The old diesel engine is a Lister double-cylinder type and is fastened down to a cement chassis in the middle of the room. On another chassis about five feet away from the motor sits the pump. Two metal pipes extend out of the pump. One runs down the well and another one goes outside to a small pool. A narrow belt runs from the motor to the pump's pulley. From where I'm sitting under the willow tree, I can see the mouth of the pipe lying on the edge of the pool—looking exactly the way I remember from the early days. Kemal has been trying to repair the motor since the morning and is covered up to his elbows with black oil and grease. Musa has been helping him. He watches closely and, when Kemal needs a hammer or a wrench, fetches it quickly and hands it to him.

I think about the time I came here months ago. Those first days are not clear in my mind and the ones that followed run into one another and blur my memory of what happened. It was late spring when I came, and now it's fall. And I'm still waiting for Ruzbeh to show up. I've sent Kemal to Shiraz a few times to see if Ruzbeh has been to the house, but he couldn't say for sure. Once a neighbor told him that they had seen the house lights on a few times, and Kemal asked them to keep an eye out.

Musa heard that a few nights ago Ruzbeh visited Mother in the village house but that he stayed only briefly and went away. I don't know what to believe. Why do you stay away, Ruzbeh? Maybe you've heard what happened to Shireen. I'm sure someone has told you by now. Is that why you don't come around? Or is it because I'm here? I wanted to wait for you at the house in Shiraz when I went to get the briefcase but was frightened by the thought of zealots finding me and dragging me to the square. Funny how I felt that I was an intruder in our own house.

A bang suddenly cuts through my thoughts. I turn and see Kemal striking a hammer, his arm flying up and down. He's determined to finish fixing the motor. When was it—a week ago?—that I signed over the deed of the Naranjestan to him and Musa? I don't know what the future will bring. But I know one thing—I couldn't stand any further destruction of the Naranjestan. Kemal worked hard to convince me to let him take control of the place. I didn't know whether he was a person to trust, but does it matter? I'm not sure of anything except that he will change this place.

Kemal was here early the day after I showed him the deed. I had never seen him here in the morning before. He had his two children with him. His wife came later. I was surprised to see a woman in this place. She began to clean the rooms right away, sweeping out the trash and the mouse droppings and taking out the empty oil cans. Kemal started to fix the broken doors and windows. I heard him telling her that later he would fix the hole in the ceiling, replace the broken glass in the windows, and paint the rooms.

Musa came around noon as usual to water his herds. I saw him watching Kemal and his family cleaning up the place. When he realized that a change was under way, that I was serious, and that Kemal was serious about taking care of the place, he stood around smoking cigarettes one after another, probably deciding whether to go or stay and work alongside Kemal. I saw them talking in the pump house. Then Musa walked away and Kemal went after him. They stopped by the small pool. The way they were pointing at each other and at the Naranjestan and the fields, it was obvious they were arguing. A few times they looked in my direction. I didn't want to get involved, figuring they needed to come to an understanding by themselves.

The next day Kemal came early again, slid open the big iron door of the pump house, and cleaned and organized the tools. Then he started to work on the motor. He took it apart and put the pistons, rings, and shaft on the ground, arranged neatly on an old blanket he had spread out.

Later in the day Musa arrived with two elderly men from the village. He told me that my signature on the deed would not be official without witnesses. The two men were very courteous. I'm sure Musa had prepared them as to who I was and in what condition they would find me. They looked very much alike in their expression, manner, and clothing—both were dressed in old gray coats and hats. One of them kept coughing. I thought they were twins, and this turned out to be the case. Musa told me that later. I could see in their eyes, from the pensive way they looked at me, that they had hundreds of questions they would have liked to ask. Questions like why I am doing this and why I am here. Or questions about America—what it was like there and whether I was planning on going back.

I looked at their tired and wrinkled faces and at their rough-skinned hands as they signed the deed and thought how those hands had worked the land day after day, turning it and sowing it, and then had been raised to the heavens, praying for rain.

After Musa and Kemal signed the deed, Kemal went back to repairing the pump and Musa and the two men went and sat on the platform. One of them was limping and walked close to the other as if he needed to lean on him to keep his balance. I couldn't take my eyes off them, two bent-over figures who had worked all their lives until no work was left in them. They shared Musa's water pipe and drank tea until noon. I could imagine them coming back to visit Musa when this place is in shape. Later Musa told me that the one with the limp plays the reed flute very well. He plays for the elderly when they are on their deathbed. The villagers believe music soothes the dying so they go out in peace.

After the two men left, Kemal showed Musa how to wash and clean the parts he had taken out of the motor. In the afternoon Kemal put the motor back together. The sun was almost setting when he announced that he was ready. He was anxious to start the motor. So was I. Musa was too, I believed, from the way he jumped to fetch the crank. But when Kemal checked the tank, there wasn't enough fuel and he decided to clean the tank and go get fuel from the city.

Today I've been sitting here against the tree since morning, watching Kemal getting the motor ready. He had to open the pump as well and clean out the rust inside. He worked on the pump until late in the afternoon, taking off the old belt and replacing it with a new one. Now, cigarette in hand, he is resting. Musa is wiping the pump with a piece of cloth. I watch impatiently.

Kemal empties a bucket of diesel fuel into the motor's tank and signals Musa to bring him the crank. He puts the crank around the shaft and, after a moment, as if saying a silent prayer, bends down beside the motor and starts to turn the crank, putting one hand on top of the motor for support. His body is bent forward and moves up and down rapidly as he turns the handle. I can hear the *hen-hen* of his breathing and the *huff-huff* of the motor, man and machine entangled in an unnatural dance. It looks like an exhausting task, and I wonder if the motor will yield to Kemal's stubbornness. I have almost given up, afraid that Kemal is about to collapse from exhaustion, when suddenly I hear a sharp *top-top* sound. Kemal takes the crank off the motor's shaft and straightens his back. The calls of the crickets are drowned out by the noise of the motor, and a coil of smoke jumps from the exhaust and unfolds against the sky.

The motor sounds like a heart beating, slow at first and then faster and faster until reaching a uniform speed—a familiar sound that I haven't heard for I don't know how long. I look at the trees, wondering if they hear it, and turn toward the fields and the desert, wishing I knew how far the sound is carrying, thinking that if Ruzbeh is out there he might hear it and come back. I wish we all were here to watch the water start flowing.

Musa and Kemal run to the pool and stare at the pipe. Only a muffled moaning sound echoes in the empty pipe. After a few moments, Kemal turns off the motor. I try to keep the sound of the motor alive in my mind and long to see the water flowing out of the pipe.

Kemal works around the pump for a while and then puts the crank around the motor's shaft again. He takes a last drag on his cigarette and with a flick of his thumb throws away the butt. He starts on the motor again, turning and turning the crank until the motor turns over. He pulls a knob and the motor gets louder and shoots smoke high into the air. But no water comes out of the pipe.

I stay where I am and watch. The same feeling fills me, the feeling of wanting the water to fly out of the pipe, wanting it to boil up like the prehistoric flood, full of energy, running over the fields and awakening the roots of the trees. But only a dry moaning sound emerges from the pipe.

Kemal turns the motor off and stares at it for a while before walking outside. He stands facing the fields, quiet, as if pleading for help from some force hidden in the open plain, then bends down, picks up a handful of dirt, and rubs his hands together to clean the grease and oil from his palms. He says something to Musa and jumps on his motorcycle and rides away.

From behind the sheets of dust set in motion by the wind, I watch the sun. It has a reddish halo and looks huge hanging at the horizon. I love this time of the day, the last hour when sun, sky, and desert are engaged in playing with colors. The yellow of the horizon changes to orange, then to scarlet, and then red as if a huge fire at the edge of the earth were slowly burning itself out, giving way to darkness. It's that time in the shift from day to evening when things take on a dreamlike quality, the eye seeing and not seeing, recognizing and not recognizing, until the power of sight is finally vanquished. I take in the passing of the time until the night creeps up around me. Then I notice the flames of a fire by the farmhouse.

"Ay, Behruz?" Musa calls. "Where are you? Come—there's a fire. Come and warm yourself."

I feel like I can't move, like my body is stuck to the tree. Musa calls again. This old man is kind to everything and everyone—even to Kemal, whom he doesn't trust. He tries to be kind to whatever has life. He has told me many times that whatever has life carries the light of God. He also has a high respect for water, believing that water is more precious than human beings, because it gives and preserves life.

The wind is starting to blow harder and colder. I stand up slowly. One of my feet is asleep. I rub it for a moment and look toward the village, where a few lights are barely visible, wondering why Kemal's wife and children didn't come today.

Musa calls again and I limp toward him. He's standing beside the fire as if paying his respects like an old Zoroastrian. I can see the reflection of the dancing flames in his eye.

"Warm yourself," he says. "Appreciate what God has granted us to bear the cold." Standing by the fire, I start to feel its warmth.

"Are you okay? You've been sitting there all day. Did you eat the food I brought you at lunchtime?"

I shake my head, remembering that I'm hungry and hadn't eaten much of the food.

Musa rubs his hands together and covers his face to warm it. "This fall cold is telling us that it's going to be a harsh winter, much worse than last year, and early too. May God help us survive the coming long cold season. The pump didn't work. It didn't bring any water up. Kemal went to the city—I think to get parts. I don't understand very much about these mechanical things."

He points to the kettle beside the fire. "When the water is hot, put some tea leaves in it and drink some. It'll warm your insides. I have to go find my herds—they've probably headed for the village by now, if they're not lost in the desert. I didn't get a chance to look after them all day. I'll come back as soon as I can and bring whatever the old woman has prepared for supper. We'll eat here together." Then he starts to look for his walking stick. "I wish I had time to warm up and have some tea, but I've got to go before jackals get to the herds."

He moves away like a shadow. I want to get up and leave as well, to disappear into the darkness that has spread out over the fields, but I don't have the courage or the energy. I lie down, the warmth of the fire slowly sinking into my bones. My eyelids start to get heavy and I hear a sound of knocking coming from the pump house.

"Behruz, wake up."

I open my eyes and see a figure standing above me with a lantern in hand lighting half his face. It takes me a moment to realize it's Musa.

"I'm back," he says. "I've brought some dinner for you. The fire has died out. I'll have to start it again."

With my eyes barely open, I watch him breaking up some branches into smaller pieces and putting them on the fire.

"Did you see the moon or were you asleep?" he asks. "It was huge, and the color of saffron. I've never seen a heavenly moon like that."

I seek out the moon, but the sky is dark and the stars few. I think of the song that Juanita used to play on her guitar.

I feel I'm knocking, she would sing, knock, knock, knocking . . . knock, knock, knocking on heaven's door.

Fifteen

I CAN'T REMEMBER EXACTLY, but it must have been a few days ago that Musa had a visitor. I was in the Naranjestan and saw someone walking with him to the platform. I'd never seen anyone like this man around here. He wasn't from the village, of that I was sure. He was clearly from the city, with his briefcase and dark suit that seemed too big for him. They talked for a long time, almost all morning. When he got up to leave, I could see that he was short like Musa, with the same narrow shoulders. He moved his hands and lowered his head like Musa. They slowly walked back and forth at the edge of the field, talking and once in a while stopping to look into the distance. It was like I was in a surrealistic world watching two homeless men across a desolated landscape who didn't know what to do, except to wait. Wait for someone to come by.

This morning Musa came and sat down beside me and began to talk as if he were telling me something he had kept inside himself for a long time. He said the man that I saw with him the other day who had come to visit was his half brother, Ebrahim, and that he was going to Shiraz to see him. He explained that Ebrahim was about to leave the country and was planning to go to Cyprus and from there to Israel to join his son, who had gone there a few years earlier. He showed me some old silver coins and an elaborate silver candelabrum looking hundreds of years old that he said had been in their family for generations. Ebrahim had left them since he was afraid he would get in trouble if at the border he were found with the silver.

"What am I to do with a candelabrum in this place?" Musa said. "I have no need for these things. He should have given them to a friend in the city, or even sold them, but he wanted to keep them in the family, maybe hoping they would get to him somehow—it's always good to be hopeful. Here I'm afraid they will be lost or stolen. I have to hide them somewhere for now." He wrapped the candelabrum and the silver in a piece of old cloth, put them in a plastic bag, and went out to bury them in the orchard.

When he came back, he made a pot of tea and showed me four old books he was taking to Ebrahim. One was a Torah that had been his father's. The others were history books. He said he had kept them hidden for many years and was hoping Ebrahim would take them.

"My father was Yusef Solimani," he told me as he sipped his tea. "First, let me tell you that I don't talk about certain things to anyone. There are things a person needs to keep within himself. I'm sure you understand that. But since I know so much about your family and you know so little of mine, I would like to tell you more. During these few months, I've come to know you. You certainly don't like to talk. You like to listen and observe. I used to be like you when I was young. But nowadays I like to talk. Maybe it's a habit of old age or being alone in this dry land, maybe it's that you are a good listener and don't ask questions."

I nodded and he went on.

"When my father was a young man he made his living by traveling from the city on his motorbike to sell clothes and jewelry in the villages. One day, when a group of village women and girls had gathered around him to try on earrings and bracelets and hold up the clothes against their bodies, he noticed a beautiful young girl with light hair, which is unusual here as you know. She was trying on a necklace. Watching her, he lost his mind for a moment and all the talk of the women went dead in his ears. When he came to, he realized that it was not only his mind but his heart that he had lost. It was a forbidden love—love between a Jewish man and a Muslim girl. And, you know, rationality loses when love emerges. That beautiful young girl, Nilufar, was my mother." I could hear the emotion in his voice. "It took a lot to convince my mother's parents to let him marry her. My father agreed to give up his religion and become a Muslim, and on top of that to live in the village. In doing this, he lost his own parents and his friends in the city. It was the most fascinating thing that had happened in the village in a long time. To have a Jew become a Muslim was a great thing for the villagers. There were big celebrations in honor of his conversion and the wedding. People came from all the surrounding villages. My granddad would tell me over and over about the wedding and the food and musicians they brought from the city."

"My grandparents loved their son-in-law. They had only my mother, no other children. My father opened up a shop in the village and traveled to the city to bring back merchandise. People came from other villages to buy from him. He had become a popular person. He would sell sewing machines on the installment plan and also teach the women how to use them. In his spare time he taught reading and writing to me and some of the other children. Every time he went to the city to get merchandise, he would come back with sweets and something special for my mother and me and books for himself. I used to show off my toys to the village kids. He used to take me to the outskirts of the village, where we would walk and he would read to me. He loved books. When he wasn't busy he sat in his shop and read. He would tell me about so many things—about the inventions that were being made and the different types of cars and machines being built in different countries. He had put a motor on his bike himself. In those days the motorcycle had not even come to the city. Can you believe that?" he asked before going on.

"When your father was here, my father made sure to come and visit him. I guess they loved to talk about the things that were happening in the city. I have a clear memory of those days. As far as your eye could see, there were fields of poppies. At that time poppy cultivation was not forbidden. The lemon grove was much smaller then. This building was not like it is now—it was only a one-room house—and they used horses to draw water from the well.

"I remember I was ten years old when a terrible thing happened that was the end of our happy family." He grew quiet for a while. "One of the villagers, a man, found out that when my father traveled to the city, he went to the synagogue there. Well, the villagers got upset, saying that he was not a real Muslim and had lied to them. My grandparents and especially my mother couldn't have cared less whether he was a Muslim or not—I know because she told me herself many times that she didn't care what God he prayed to as long as he had a belief. No one had ever seen anything like it. People were so angry. They put fire to the shop and everything inside. I can still see the flames and the dark smoke. It was the darkest smoke I'd ever seen."

His voice was tense with emotion, and I felt very uncomfortable and sad.

"I'm sorry, Musa," I said. "You don't have to tell me if you don't want to."

"I want to. I want you to hear this. I've told you that I owe a lot to your parents. You know I always had a job at Naranjestan. I used to help your father with the accounting during the harvest, which was only a few months, but he would pay me a full year's salary. Ruzbeh was kind enough to continue and offer me the same. But I really owe your father for something grave and that's what I want to tell you about.

"After the shop was burned down, a few of the villagers, 'the troublemakers,' were going to kill my father, but he managed to get away somehow. They saw him heading for the Naranjestan, and they followed him, but it was his luck that your father, God rest his soul, was there at the time. My grandfather told me that your father stood in front of the door of the farmhouse and said, 'Anyone who wants to enter must step over my dead body. This is my property and if you don't leave now, you'll be dead!'"

I looked at Musa in silence, thinking about my father. I knew he had no tolerance for wrongdoing and that he told us many times to be strong and stand up for ourselves.

"Anyway," Musa continued, "that's the reason that some villagers called your father a 'Jew lover.' It was forgotten for years, until, at the time of the revolution, when all sorts of strange things were happening, some of the villagers used this as an excuse to take the Naranjestan."

He poured two more cups of tea. There were many questions I would have liked to ask, like where he was while all this was happening. I decided not to intrude and let him talk.

"It must have been hard for my father to give up the city and his family and friends. He had a radio and listened to the news. But I know he missed being part of the conversations that must have been going on among his friends."

He drank his tea quickly and poured another cup before speaking again. "You know, the burning of the shop was the doing of a few stupid men in the village. During the month of Ramadan, a mullah would come to the village and talk about the historical problems between Jews and Muslims at the time of Muhammad the Prophet and the famous wars between Medina and Mecca."

He filled up my teacup. "Maybe you know all this," he said.

"No, tell me," I said.

"Well, Prophet Muhammad had many wars—or, as it is said, was faced with many wars. I don't exactly know how many—seventy or so. One famous one was the Battle of Ohod, when Abu Sufyan, the head of Mecca, attacked Medina and many Muslims were killed. Muhammad was injured and his uncle Hamzeh was killed by a spear. Hind, the wife of Abu Sufyan, was participating in this war. Her father had been killed by Hamzeh in the previous battle, and she was seeking revenge. It's written that after Hamzeh fell, she personally opened his body, pulled out his liver, and took a bite out of it. She is famous for this and is called 'Hind the liver eater.' I don't know why I'm telling you this, the story has always made me shiver . . . Anyway, there was the Battle of Khandagh—the trench—which I wanted to tell you about. At one time, there was the danger of Medina's being attacked by the Meccans. Salman the Persian, one of the Prophet's disciples, came up with the idea of digging a trench around the city, a defensive tactic used by the Persians and Byzantines. It was in this war that the relationship between Jews and Muslims went sour. The Jews didn't want to help in financing the war and later were accused of spying. It is written that after the war, five hundred or more Jews were put to death by Muslims and the rest had to leave Medina. They went to the rich village of Khaybar to live with another Jewish tribe. A few years later, this village was attacked by Muslims and was taken, and all the Jews had to leave.

"It was these wars that the mullah would talk about during Ramadan, and the result was devastating for my family. After all the trouble, my father never came back to the village. When my mother died a few years later, my grandparents from the city came and got me, but I was miserable in the city and didn't want to stay because my father's new wife—Ebrahim's mother—was a mean woman. Ebrahim was a year old when I came back. I was safe here because of my grandfather. Also, because I didn't stay in the city, people saw it as a sign that I had nothing to do with my father or his faith and would grow up a Muslim in the village. Later, when I was older, I would go and see my father and Ebrahim once in a while, but we didn't really know each other well. By then my father was weak and fragile, but he had his ears to the radio day and night, listening to the news about the great war in Europe and the fate of millions of his people. We were very far from the war, but there were many disturbing stories and rumors around."

He stopped and reflected for a long time. "Well," he said finally, "now Ebrahim is trying to convince me to go with him to Israel. I just don't have the desire anymore. I did at one time, when I was younger. I could imagine going to the big cities, to the Persian Gulf, or even to another country. But time passed and I never left. It was much easier to go to Israel those days. Today it's a different story, as I'm sure you know."

I looked at him and thought of the Palestinian friends I used to have in the United States and how passionately they talked about their homeland. "I can't go back," I still remember one of them saying. "I'm not allowed to go back."

"Behruz," he said after a moment, a curious look in his eye, "have you ever read One Thousand and One Nights and wished that you could meet Scheherazade? That one summer night under the stars of this old desert she would appear to you, like one of those magical things that happen in stories and make you wonder about the wonders of the world? I have. Many nights I have wondered and wished for her to appear and take me to a fantastic place outside of this world."

For a moment I wondered what sort of place he was imagining. Was that his promised land—a place of tranquility that humans have been searching for since they gained consciousness? A magical world existing only in the mind?

"I used to visit Ebrahim once in a while," he said, sipping the last of his tea. "When I went to the city I would go by his shop and try to spend a couple of hours with him. The day you sent me to the city to bring back your father's briefcase, I went there. Ebrahim believes that I'm still a Jew, even though I was brought into this world by a non-Jewish mother and have never practiced the religion. He's always talked abut the Promised Land, but there was no reason to leave our birthplace and go live there. But, now, after the revolution, things are different and I don't blame him if he wants to leave. I actually hope he can go. Because he's a believer. He needs to see the place and should be able to do what he wishes. He wants me to go with him and says that he has worked everything out and all we need to do is to get to Cyprus. From there it is very easy to go to Jerusalem."

I wished I could have met Ebrahim when he came to visit Musa— two brothers, yet so different. One staying and one striving to go. I would have wished him luck reaching the Promised Land.

"As for going to Jerusalem," Musa said, "well, I've seen enough for one lifetime, enough of good and bad, of people not getting along and then of unique people like your father. There's no need for me or my wife to go anywhere. Pain, loneliness, greed, sadness. The nature of humans is the same anywhere you go. There's no getting away from it. You probably know that too," he said, looking at me. "This brother of mine is a believer—but me, I don't know what I am, really. I only know to be kind to all fellow human beings."

Sixteen

I HAVE DECIDED TO GO SEE Mother at the village house. Maybe it's because of last night's dream that I can't get her out of my mind. I struggle to keep the bad images at bay, try in vain to fight them with more pleasant thoughts but can't keep from thinking about the dream.

. . . There was a fire burning on the hillside and hundreds of people, all with sheets of paper in hand, pushed and shoved to get to me. I signed sheet after sheet, handing them over, not caring who grabbed them. They took the papers and threw them on the bonfire. With each sheet, the fire flared. I recognized many people in the crowd. The two brothers Musa brought to the Naranjestan, Kemal with his wife and children. Musa was there with his brother, suitcase in hand. Haji Zaman, white as a ghost, chuckled in a horrifying manner, his dentures rattling together. At the edge of the crowd a tall man in a bright-yellow outfit holding a rifle was trying to keep order. Father and Mother stood apart from the others and stared at me, grinning. Mother's hair was disheveled and she waved me toward her. Suddenly, sensing the heat on my face and hands, I realized I was about to be pushed into the fire . . .

I'm tired from being in the orchard among the old trees and go to the well and draw a bucket of water to wash. I don't know how Mother will react to my visit. She may not be pleased to see me with long hair and a beard. I wish there were some flowers in the fields I could pick or that I had some sweets to take to her. Chocolates would be perfect—she loved the ones I brought from America.

I wait until late afternoon and then put on the clean clothes I asked Kemal to get me a few days ago and start off. It doesn't take long to get there. The village, with its sand-colored mud-brick houses all cramped so close together, seems to have grown out of the earth. When I get nearer, I start to walk quickly, hoping not to attract any attention, especially since the briefcase I'm carrying makes me look like an outsider. I'm afraid that children will gather around trying to figure out who I am and what I'm doing there or that dogs will attack me. I listen but hear only a lone dog barking. The village seems empty, as if all the people had picked up and left.

The house sits at the entrance to the village and is the only two-story house in the area. The large yard used to have a garden and a small pool that was filled by water drawn from the well. My grandfather built it. It was his summer and fall house. Every year he would come from the city to oversee the harvest. Father didn't like to stay here. He preferred to stay in the Naranjestan and built the farmhouse there.

I walk into the yard, and when I am halfway to the house, an old woman, bent and wearing dark clothes, looks at me for a moment and then rushes toward me. "Oh, Ruzbeh," she says excitedly, "where have you been? We've been waiting for you."

When she steps closer, she looks puzzled for a moment. "Ah, Behruz," she says, "it's you." She tries to smile, but I see disappointment on her face. "Come in, come in"

It's Bibi Khanom, Shireen's mother. She seems much older than when she came to see me in the city after I got back from the United States. Seeing her, I think again about the many problems my affair with Shireen has caused and wish I hadn't come.

"How are you, dear?" she asks as she hugs and kisses me.

"Salaam, Bibi. I'm fine, thank you. How are you?"

"I'm okay. Praised be God." I can hear her labored breathing. "Where is Ruzbeh? He hasn't been here for weeks. And where have you been?"

"I've been at the Naranjestan. I haven't seen Ruzbeh either."

"Musa's wife told me you were staying there. Why did you wait so long to come and visit? Come, your mother is in her room."

I follow her down the long hallway where the sun shines in through large windows. The panes of colored glass at the top of the windows remind me of how we liked to play in the hallway when we were children, stepping on patches of color on the floor cast down through the windows. Bibi leads me through the sea of colors and opens a door. I hesitate and then step in.

The room is large and the blinds are drawn. Mother is sitting up in bed, propped up by big pillows and looking at an album of family pictures. She closes the album and puts it beside her when she sees me come in. On the table by the bed are piles of books and papers that she brought with her when she came here to escape the nightly bomb raids on the city.

"Ah, Ruzbeh-joon, aamedi. Kojá boodi? Nime joonam kardi. Bia, bia pish-am"—You're back. Where have you been? You're killing me by staying away. Come, come to me.

"Hello, Maman," I say, "It's Behruz. How are you?"

She opens her eyes in disbelief but tells me to sit down. She looks the way I saw her in my dream, her white hair uncombed and looking like she's seen a scorpion in her bed. It's not like her not to take care of herself, to be so unaware of her beauty. Her hands shake as she holds them out toward me. My heart sinks, seeing her like this. I set the briefcase on the floor, sit on the edge of the bed, and hold her hand. She pulls me to her and kisses me.

"Don't you think you're a bit too old to play that boyhood game on me," she says. "Do you think your own mother can't tell you two apart?"

I want to tell her I'm not Ruzbeh and not playing any game, but she goes on talking. I wonder how she could be confused. She never confused me with Ruzbeh, even when we tried to trick her. I push my hair back from my forehead hoping she can see my face better or at least notices that there is no sign of injury there.

"Ruzbeh, where have you been? Where is Shireen? Why didn't you bring her?"

I feel empty and useless and don't dare to utter a word about Shireen, not knowing what she knows or what her mental state is.

"I'm so happy to see you." A soft smile lights up her face. "What is this long hair and beard?" Then tears come to her eyes.

"I want to go back home," she says. "Back to Shiraz. I don't know what's become of our house. I want to go. I don't care if there is a war and the city is being bombed. Did you go to the Naranjestan? I've heard Behruz is there. Let's go get him and go home."

"Maman, I'm Behruz."

"Tell me about Shireen." She goes on as if not hearing me. "She hasn't come for I don't know how long. I think everyone is hiding something from me."

I sit still, feeling the warmth of her hand.

"You know Behruz came here the other day. He came when I was asleep. I was taking a nap and when I opened my eyes he was standing right there." She points to the door. "Can you understand that? He was standing there looking at me without saying a word and as soon as I opened my eyes he walked away."

I wonder if Ruzbeh was here after all. Musa mentioned that he had been, but Bibi said she hadn't seen him recently. Now I don't know what to think.

I can see she has been alone here too long. After a long silence, she asks, "Do you know what happened to them?"

"Who, Maman? Who are you talking about?"

"They were innocent young girls. Why were they taken away?"

I realize she is talking about her students at the girls' high school where she used to teach. After the revolution, Mother resigned her teaching post to protest the arrest of a few young girls accused of antirevolutionary activities and the expulsion of others for being Baha'i. I wonder if she often thinks about her teaching days. Maybe she talks to Bibi about the way things turned out and what she could have done differently.

"He wanted to sell the place."

"Who? What place, Maman?"

"Your father. He wanted to sell the Naranjestan. How could he? I didn't let him. The place that I love, full of memories of my children. Do you remember the summer we went north to the Caspian Sea? You twins loved the sea. Would you like to go again? What a wonderful trip it was. We should go to the sea again."

She goes on talking, jumping from one thing to another until she exhausts herself. She closes her eyes and her face grows peaceful. I hold her hand, listening to her calm breathing. I want her to be well, to be the way she always was, hopeful and full of energy. And serious, she was always serious. I need to do something for her. I should talk to Musa. I don't know how long I've been sitting when I feel her hand move. She shifts a little but stays asleep. On the wall beside the bed are pictures of the family. In one Ruzbeh and Shireen are standing by a rosebush and in another one all of us are together. From one of the pictures Father looks down on me as if to ask, why are you here? Haven't you done enough damage? You should let your mother be. You should leave her in peace.

I break into a cold sweat and tear my eyes from his gaze.

Mother's hand feels damp in my grip. "I'm sorry, Maman," I whisper. "I'm sorry for all the misfortunes that happened to us. I know I haven't been much help to you. Please forgive me. Forgive as you always have. Be strong the way you have always been. I'll do my best to find Ruzbeh"—*and to find Shireen,* I add silently to myself.

Slowly I take my hand out of hers, kiss her on the forehead, and leave the warm and stuffy room.

I don't see Bibi but hear what I think is a soft sobbing coming from one of the rooms. I'm in the middle of the yard when I hear her call from a window.

"Wait, Behruz! Where are you going? Stay for dinner."

I walk back and stand under the window. "Sorry, Bibi, I have to go. Thank you for taking care of Maman, and I'm sorry for everything. Sorry for all the problems. I'll send Musa to see you. I'll see if I can arrange it so you and Maman can go to Shiraz."

"Good. It will be better for her," she says, and I leave quickly, walking back the same dusty path toward the Naranjestan. It's that time of day when evening is approaching and your vision enters into a state of doubt since whatever you see may not be what it appears to be. The villagers have a name for this time of the day, calling it the hour of the *goorg-o-mish*—wolf-sheep—after the sheep appearing in the distance that could actually be a wolf.

Seventeen

A T NIGHT I HEAR THE JACKALS hunting for prey. It starts with one high-pitched wail, then another follows and another, their contagious enthusiasm speeding across the barren fields. Some nights I have heard them in the Naranjestan and even near the house. They must smell my bloody urine in the orchard and are aware that I am weakening and anticipating my collapse.

I was awake all night, pacing back and forth between the house and the pump house. I felt like walking away but didn't dare to brave the desert night. The dark was intense and the stars very low. Ruzbeh would have loved it and said it was a good night to catch a star. He would have told me to stand on my toes and stretch out my arm. "You must feel it," he would insist. "Feel it in your heart, raise your arm high and close your fist quickly, then bring it down and see if you've caught one."

The jackals were hollering in the distance and once I thought I heard a cry, someone crying, "Noooooooooooooooo." Or was it in my imagination? It was sudden and piercing like a cry giving way to a silence so heavy as if the whole existence had stopped before the explosion of stones toward a white-shrouded figure buried to the waist in the center of the square.

Who can explain why savagery is so entangled with this land? Or how cruelty and violence can reinvent themselves time after time so that they have no end? Centuries ago, old Zoroaster walked these lands and told us of the struggle between light and darkness, encouraging us to practice kindness and good deeds so that light would be victorious over darkness. Was nothing learned from him?

Is it possible that Shireen's gentleness won over the wrath of the stones? Musa said he heard that she managed to pull herself out of the pit and so must be forgiven since, according to Islamic law, she is considered innocent. But if this is really what happened and Shireen is alive, where is she and what has happened to her? And why haven't I heard anything from Kemal?—Kemal, who always brags of his connections in the city and brings news of what is happening there. Why hasn't he brought me any news of her?

I paced with Shireen's image in my mind. I missed her and wanted her next to me, even though I knew I didn't have the right to think that way. I wanted her, even though I didn't deserve her.

O sweet heaven, if she has survived, what kind of condition can she be in? Are her bones broken? Does she need help?

I paced until night picked up its dark veil and went away and everything was as it had been—the thirsty orchard, the silent pump house, and the village in the distance awakening to the sound of roosters and dogs. I stood at the edge of the well in the early-morning sun, my shadow broken where it went inside the well and emerged to stretch out toward fields as far as my eyes could follow it.

At my usual place beside the dry streambed, I can see Musa at the end of the fields, driving his herds out to graze. Yesterday when he came back from the city, it was too late to ask him about his trip and whether he had seen his brother.

Kemal arrives with his son and daughter behind him on the motorcycle. He waves and goes toward the pump house. I want to ask him if he found out anything about Shireen or Ruzbeh but don't. I know that if he had any news, he would come straight to me. In the past few days he's been engaged in his work, forgetting about everything else. It makes me wonder whether all his kindness was aimed only at getting the orchard. He hasn't sat with me the way he used to or brought me anything to drink. All his efforts and thoughts have been on the pump.

I hear him calling to his children, "Amir, Golboo—don't go too far and don't go near the well."

I watch them running around the pump house and through the lemon trees and can't help worrying when they are here. A few days ago I kicked a piece of dry earth and a bunch of scorpions rushed out, small shiny creatures with a sickly yellow color, their tails coiled up and their legs moving quickly. They ran in all directions. One rushed toward me, either deliberately or out of confusion. I was shaken and felt paralyzed, but it changed direction and moved away. Later I kept thinking about Musa's story of the prince who had been stung by a scorpion in spite of being kept in a glass palace. I must tell Kemal to caution the children.

I want to call to them. "Hey, little ones—come here. Come here and sit with me. Come and I'll tell you a tale, the tale of this Naranjestan. Now it is dry and dying, but when I was your age, it was green and fruitful, and I used to run all around just like you." But what is the use of their knowing that? Let them see the Naranjestan the way it is now. Why should I turn their minds to a past they have no conception of? They'll remember it as it is now unless their father is able to bring water out of the well. Then in the spring they will see the Naranjestan in front of them as green as I see it in my memory.

Sunset is approaching and Kemal is still working on the pump. His wife came around noontime to bring us lunch and make tea. The children came close only when they brought me rice and *kabab*, handing it to me and running away before I got a chance to say a word.

What a long day it's been. And how tired I am. I feel as if I've been waiting all my life for the day the pump starts and the water begins to flow. I see Kemal getting ready to start the motor, the old Lister diesel engine, whose origin dates to the development of the early steam engine.

It's said that the idea for the steam engine came to James Watt when he saw an early pressure cooker made by Denis Papin, who thought of it while watching the lid of a cooking pot rattling from the force of the steam. Here in this land we have for centuries watched the lid of the kettle dance when water is heated for tea, and no one ever had such a thought. What of our inventions has changed people's lives for the better? Here we are, a people of copiers and counterfeiters, who copy from the West and don't even copy well. Even our religion was introduced to us. We are a people of the past, always blabbering that we had the first empire in the world, that we had great kings and ruled from India to the Mediterranean and Egypt. But what about now? What about our place in modern history? I remember my days in America when I roamed the libraries, finding all sorts of books about pre-Islamic Persia, books on Persia as a cradle of civilization, the ancient Aryans, and the clash of Greeks and Persians, and then those on Muhammad and the expansion of Islam, but what do we have now? The universities nonfunctioning, the oil industry a bombed-out ruin, and civil law abandoned.

Kemal fixes the handle to the motor's shaft. My heart starts to beat faster. I stand up to see better. I want to call out, "Make it work, Kemal! Put your sweat and blood into it and make the motor run!" He spits on the palm of his hand, bends down, and wraps his fingers around the handle. As he turns it, his body makes a circular motion and his breathing mixes with the *huff-huff* of the motor. Then suddenly the motor starts to chug with a *top-top* sound and sends a fountain of black smoke into the clear sky. My eyes turn to the pool. A heavy muffled sound echoes in the mouth of the pipe. Musa runs out and puts the palm of his hand on the mouth of the pipe, covering it and then lifting his palm slightly and letting the air be sucked in as if giving it mouth-to-mouth resuscitation.

Kemal looks across toward Musa and increases the flow of the fuel. The motor wails louder and sends more smoke into the sky. The vacuumlike sound grows louder as Musa covers and uncovers the mouth of the pipe. Kemal increases and decreases the flow of the fuel to the motor. Then all at once the sound recedes inside the pipe as if it is rushing to the heart of the earth and a sudden shine of water jumps out, at first in broken gulps, then flowing continuously.

"*Aab!*"—water! Musa yells toward Kemal.

Kemal runs to the pool, the children behind him. He puts his hand under the pipe as if he can't believe it is really water pouring out. The children and Musa do the same, holding their hands under the water and staring at it. It looks like they are prepared to stay there forever so that it won't cease to flow. All of them move around the pool as if performing a ritual water dance.

Seeing the water and listening to its sound as it pours into the pool makes me excited and happy. But I stay where I am by the dry streambed awaiting the flow of the water, and it does not take long until I hear a hissing sound and then see the water crawling closer, pushing dirt and debris ahead of it. When it reaches me, I start to walk alongside the flow. A breeze starts to blow through the trees, and the branches sway as if they are bowing to the arrival of water. I imagine the tree roots are beginning to sense the murmuring of the passing water. As the water stretches out, its cloudiness clears and it becomes a mirror for the orchard and the sky.

Eighteen

I WALK ALONG WITH THE WATER through the Naranjestan and toward the open fields, which at this time of year should be plowed and ready to be sown with winter wheat. Behind I can hear the *top-top* of the motor and the laughter of Musa and Kemal and the children beside the pool. I watch for a few minutes and then am drawn back to the water. The flow has picked up speed as if in a hurry to get to the end of the fields and push back the desert. It extends well ahead of me now. As I walk farther, the voices fade but I can still hear the sound of the motor. When I reach the end of the Naranjestan, following the stream, I see something moving. When I get closer, I can make out the shape of a person sitting beside the stream. It looks like a man. In a few minutes I reach him. His head is bent down and he is watching the water splashing around his bare feet.

I pick up my pace. "Ruzbeh," I cry out. "Is that you? Please stay where you are. Stay there!"

My voice scratches my throat as if I hadn't spoken for years. I reach him and stop. My heart racing, "Oh dear God," I say with tears in my eyes.

"Ruzbeh-*jan*. Ruzbeh—it's me, Behruz."

He doesn't move or look up. Like a child with a shiny new toy, he is playing with the water, bringing it up, cupped in his hands, and letting it pour out through his fingers while he whispers something I can't make out. I move closer slowly, worried that I will scare him away.

He looks at me briefly. He's thin and has a long beard. I know he recognizes me and think he might get up and go away, but he turns back to the water. I approach slowly and sit down beside him. I can see my reflection beside his in the water—Ruzbeh and Behruz, two gaunt figures with tousled hair.

I put my arm around his shoulder.

"Ruzbeh," I say, breaking down in tears. "Where did you go? Where have you been?" I hold him tighter and he returns my embrace. "Dear brother. I've been looking for you. Oh, dear Ruzbeh, I love you. I've missed you so much. Please don't go away again."

He raises his head. The scar on his forehead, a faint line the color of the desert, makes my heart ache. He points toward the fields and the irrigation ditches.

"I've been looking for you. I'm so happy I found you." I kiss him again. "Tell me, are you okay? How are you?"

He looks at me as if searching his memory. His eyes—those eyes that I know so well—have a watery look to them. When he was excited or was hiding something, I always could see it in his eyes. I have no idea if he knows about Shireen or will be willing even to talk to me. I stand up and wipe my eyes. Ruzbeh goes on murmuring as if singing a lullaby, calling to Shireen to come and sit beside him.

I watch him looking at Shireen, talking to Shireen, and can almost see her in her red dress, wading in the water and tossing her head as she talks. I wait for a while, my cheeks streaked with tears. I kneel beside him and put my hand under his chin, bringing his head up so I can look into his eyes. I see that he knows it's me. Our eyes cloud with memories. We were always like this, knowing each other's feelings without saying a word.

"Ruzbeh-*jan*—get up, let's go back. You can't stay out here anymore. Let's go back to the Naranjestan. Everything is taken care of. Musa and Kemal are there and will take care of you."

For a moment his eyes drift in the direction I'm pointing, and then he turns away. Cupping my hands, I fill them with water. He lets me wash his face. I can feel the lump of broken bone in his forehead. It's the first time I've touched his injury. I sit watching the water for a while before washing his feet. Then I wash myself. I put his boots beside him and ask him to put them on. He does, still murmuring to himself.

I know he is like this when he doesn't take his medicine. He has severe headaches and his depression deepens, and all he can do is walk aimlessly. I wonder whether it was the sound of the motor pump that drew him here.

I help him to put his jacket on and shake the dust off him.

"Let's go to the Naranjestan. Enough wandering. You must be tired. I am—very tired. The water is coming from there. Kemal fixed the pump." We turn to go back.

"You haven't been taking your medicine, have you?" I ask.

He shakes his head.

"We'll fix that. I am sure Maman has some. She was always good at keeping some extra for you."

He nods absentmindedly.

"We'll go and see Maman tomorrow. She's waiting for you. She needs you with her. I went to visit her today."

"Tell me, Ruzbeh," I ask after a while. "Before you went away, at least you came back once in a while. Someone always knew where you were, but this time, no one knew."

He pauses as if trying to gather his thoughts. "I wanted to come to the Naranjestan," he says at last, "but I couldn't."

"Did you go to Maman and Bibi or to the house in Shiraz?"

"I wanted to, but I couldn't"

"Why?"

"There's nothing left."

I know he must be talking about Shireen. I don't say a word. Can I say it's my fault what happened? Or was it his doing as well, the way he ran away from her and left her alone? We walk in silence.

Finally he says, "I heard Shireen disappeared. I know it was my fault."

"No. It wasn't your fault," I say, my voice choking. "We'll find her. Do you know where she is?"

He doesn't answer.

"I'm sorry, Ruzbeh. You don't need to worry now. I should have tried harder to find you. I'll take care of you." Tears come to my eyes at seeing him this way.

As we walk side by side through the lemon grove I remember the innocent days when we used to run around here and can't stop thinking that as an adult I should have been more responsible, I should've taken better care of him and Shireen. I was self-absorbed and didn't think about the consequences of our actions at a time when the consequences were so grave and the price of being foolish so high.

I feel an emptiness inside me. When I look around there is a murmuring in the air as if the trees, the water, the breeze, all are telling me that something is missing.

I stop short.

"Please forgive me, Ruzbeh. I can't come with you. There is something important I have to do. I have to go to the city. I have to go and look for Shireen."

A faint smile appears on his lips. He nods.

"Promise me that you will go to the farmhouse. Things have changed there. Musa and Kemal are there now. The old man has been taking care of me. He'll take care of you too. Tell him I've gone to the city. You need to go and get your pills from Maman. She'll be very pleased to see you. She needs to see you. Bibi as well. I want you to stay there. Musa will help you. Will you promise me?"

He nods.

I draw him to me and hug him hard, feeling the warmth of his body. I touch his skin. I kiss him, kiss his eyes, and hug him again, wanting to give him my last bit of warmth—my last bit of energy, wanting to give him all the life that is left in me.

I start to walk away but go only a few steps and turn to hug him again. It feels so much like the day, almost eight years ago, when

I left for America. I hold him tight, wanting to repair the rupture between us.

He smiles and then starts walking toward the farmhouse, still murmuring to Shireen as if she were there beside him. I wish I could promise him that I will find her, that I will bring her back.

I watch him, a thin shadow, walk through the old lemon trees toward Musa and the others. I wait until I'm sure Musa sees him, then turn around and start out across the desert, still hearing the words of the lullaby Ruzbeh was singing.

Nineteen

T HE DESERT SKY IS BRIGHT with stars. Cold saturates the
night and I keep walking, not knowing exactly where I am,
just hoping that I'm going in the right direction and will soon be on
the road by the mountainside that leads to Shiraz. Maybe I should
have gone back with Ruzbeh and asked Kemal to take me into the
city, but I didn't want him or the old man to stop me from going.
All this has nothing to do with them, and I didn't want to put them
in any danger.

The sudden shriek of jackals startles me. I stop for a moment,
thinking that they have seen me and are close by. I start to run—I
don't know how far or in what direction—until I hear the sound of
music ahead. I think I'm hearing things, but when I reach the top of
the hill I can see a fire burning below and the dark shapes of people
moving near the flames. A woman is singing, accompanied by the
jingle-jangle of a tambourine. I realize they are Gypsies, maybe the
same family I saw one evening when they came to the lemon grove
to draw water from the well.

I stand there wishing I could warm myself by the fire. Then I decide to go down, thinking that I should take the risk if I don't want to be attacked by jackals or frozen by the desert cold. I start down the hill and then hear dogs barking. They rush toward me, stopping just a few steps away barking furiously. The music stops, and two men approach.

"Who's there?" a man asks.

"Hush, hush," someone calls out to the dogs. "Get back."

"Who's there?" The man asks again.

"Behruz Pirzad."

One of the men comes closer and the other tries to get the dogs to stop barking.

"Come. Come," he says, motioning to me.

I follow him to the campground, where a group of women and children sitting beside the fire look at me in silence.

"Come, *khosh aamadi*—welcome," he says. "Sit and warm yourself."

He points to the kilim that is spread out beside the fire and I sit down. The women get up and disappear into a nearby dark tent. The other two men also leave. The dogs, having done their duty, lie quiet beside the fire with their heads on their paws. I realize how shaken I was when they came at me.

"I'm Davood Herati," the man says with a smile, his gold tooth shining. He's a small man with thick eyebrows and a prominent nose. In the light of the flames, he doesn't look old, but his hair is white. I notice that he is staring at me. "I can't believe it. You're just like your twin brother, Ruzbeh. We've known him for many years. He was staying with us for a while and left for the Naranjestan just this afternoon. At first I thought he had changed his mind and come back. But our dogs don't bark at him, they know him."

The children watch me. A little girl comes closer and looks at me before speaking, "Salaam, Ruzbeh, are you going to stay with us?"

I take her hand and smile. "I'm Ruzbeh's brother. My name is Behruz."

Another girl and two boys come closer as well. They stare at me as if not believing what I'm saying.

Davood calls out. "Ay, Zinat—where are you, woman? Bring some food and tea for our guest."

I turn to the little girl. "What's your name?"

"Abrisham," she says after a while.

"Ah. What a beautiful name. Abrisham. You're the only girl I know who's name means 'silk.'"

They look at one another and giggle.

"You better get up and go to bed now," Davood tells the children. "It's late and we have to start early tomorrow."

"Where were you going at this time of night?" He turns to me.

"To Shiraz. I was trying to get to the city road."

A woman brings over a tray. She is so quiet that I see her only as she turns to go.

"You must be hungry and tired," Davood says as he puts down the tray in front of me. "Here's some food. Please eat."

I take some dates and a piece of bread.

"We've known your brother for many years," he says to me. "He used to give us jobs during harvesttime. We picked lemons and oranges for him."

He smiles after each comment as if he wants me to feel comfortable, and my fears start to evaporate. I wish they would start singing again but know they won't. They probably don't want to put themselves in danger, since the government forbids playing music and singing.

Again in a soft voice Davood addresses the children. "Didn't I say go to bed? We need to be up early in the morning. It will be a long day of walking."

"It's good you came this way," he says to me. "There's nothing around here. You could freeze from the cold at this time of the year. We're on our yearly trip south, where it's warmer, and are going to the city bazaar to buy what we need for the road."

A young woman brings a pot of tea with cups and puts them down in front of us. In the glow cast over her face by the fluttering flames, I see that she has a tattoo on her chin, but she straightens up so quickly I can't make out what it is.

I eat in silence. On the other side of the hearth another woman is spreading out a blanket close to the fire. From the way Davood gestures to her, I guess that it is for me. A few people are sleeping beside the tent, covered with blankets.

Davood puts a cup of tea in front of me and takes one for himself. "You can't get to the road at this time of night. You'd better sleep here." He points toward the blankets spread on the ground. "You must be tired. Get a good night's sleep and tomorrow you can come with us. The road isn't far, less than an hour away, and there are many cars and trucks going to the city. We like walking—it's cheaper," he says with a short laugh. "We just gather our things and hit the road, the way our parents used to do."

He puts a piece of hard sugar in his mouth and drinks his tea in quick sips. "Don't worry about anything—you're safe here. Sleep. I'll wake you in the morning."

I take off my shoes, the ones Kemal gave me some time ago that are not good for walking and have left my feet throbbing. I lie down, enjoying the sensation of stretching my legs out beside the fire and hoping sleep will come soon. Everything about these people seems natural—the way they took me in and the women knew just what to do, bringing food and tea and preparing a place for me to sleep. I think of Ruzbeh and feel happy to know that he wasn't alone in the desert or in danger. He was with these kind people and now I've stumbled across their path as well. It's hard for me to believe that there are still Gypsies in this part of the country. I knew about the nomadic Qashqai and Basseri tribes in southern Iran but thought that the Gypsies had all settled in the cities. I've seen them in the streets, telling fortunes, begging, or selling odd things. Even though people mistrust them, they would gather around to hear their fortunes.

I wake up to the barking of dogs and a cool morning breeze. It takes me a moment to realize where I am. Women are hurrying around, carrying things out of three black tents that stand aslant the hill not far from one another. A child is crying in front of one of them. It comes to me that I dreamt about Juanita. We were traveling in a car somewhere in the Midwest and she was explaining something, but

I don't remember much of the dream. I wonder what she would think of these people and their jet-black tents of woven goat hair, so unlike the Native Americans with their painted animal-skin teepees decorated with bird feathers.

I hear the call of mountain doves and realize we're on the side of the mountain with the vast arid plain in front of us. In the distance there are two dark spots that might be the village and the lemon grove. I must have been totally lost last night to have come in this direction.

Davood appears from behind one of the tents. "Good morning," he says cheerfully. "I was waiting for you to wake up. The women have boiled some water so you can wash. It's our custom to wash and wear our best clothes to start our yearly journey."

I walk with him to one of the tents. He holds the front flap open and asks me to go in. A large pot of water is set on a stone tripod over a small fire.

"Sit and wash yourself," Davood says pointing to a boulder with a bowl beside it. "I'll be back in a while."

Inside the tent, the dim rays of the sun shower in through the woven black canvas of the tent like thousands of needles. I take off my shirt and pour bowls of water on my head and shoulders. The warm water rushing down my back tickles my skin. I enjoy the sensation, not knowing the last time I had a warm bath. I wash the best I can and dry myself with the towel Davood left in the corner of the tent. When I step outside the tent, the morning sun is bright and I have to shade my eyes for a moment.

"I think you should let me cut your hair," Davood says as he comes over. "You'll be in trouble with long hair in the city—the *passdars* will pick you up right away. Having a beard is fine, but long hair is forbidden. I can give you a shave as well." He smiles and I nod in agreement.

I should have thought about the danger myself. He tells me to sit on a rock a few steps away from the tent, then goes away and comes back with an old case. When he opens it, I see pairs of scissors and hair clippers all neatly arranged. He puts the towel around my neck in a practiced way and cuts my hair while the activities of the camp go on around us. The women are putting their household items in big cloth bags. The young men are tearing down the tents, piling up the long poles and folding the tents. The children are busy rolling up the kilims and blankets. I don't see any sign of the dogs that were barking at me last night.

"I was born in Afghanistan," Davood goes on talking. "Many years ago—in Herat. My father came to this part of the world when I was only a few months old. Some people think we are from the big Qashqai tribe. But we're Gypsies. In those days life was different. In the villages we repaired farm equipment, sharpened tools, and traded animals with the villagers, but things have changed. There are more tractors and combines nowadays and not as much need for fixing tools. We're three families and all related. Our numbers used to be greater, but some of us settled in Shiraz and other towns where the young people do odd jobs."

After he finishes cutting my hair, he shaves me slowly and carefully. Then he hands me a small, worn-out mirror.

"Here, see how much younger you look."

I haven't looked at myself for months and can't believe how thin my face looks. A young boy brings me something to eat—bread and dates and hot tea. Two other boys take down the tent and fold it in a quick and professional manner.

Davood helps to load the last donkey. All their belongings are on four donkeys and a horse. On one donkey, between the tent poles hanging horizontally on either side, an old woman sits holding a bundle and a small child. Another is loaded with two huge sacks and a few pots and pans tied together with a rope going through the handles. There are more children than I thought and four men including Davood. Two of the women have babies tied on their backs. Unlike the city women, who dress in black chadors and wear gold jewelry, they are wearing clothes decorated with colored beads and have on silver necklaces and earrings.

When everything is ready and we start to move on, suddenly the three dogs appear from nowhere and run ahead of us. I walk beside Davood. The children who were sitting with me last night follow behind. "The city isn't far," he says. "We'll be there by early afternoon, but it's only half an hour to the city road. You can go on by car or bus when we get there."

Once in a while he goes around to check the loads and talk to his sons and then comes back to walk with me.

"Do you like moving around like this?" I ask.

"Yes. I like it, but not my family. My sons with young children would like to live in the city, for the future of the children. I like to move around and be in the mountains and close to nature, but I don't know how long I can do it. I am getting on in years. I'm sixty years old and can't walk as well as I used to." He gestures toward his wife, who is on one of the donkeys. "She can't walk on trips like this anymore; her knees gave out a few months ago. This might have to be our last move. Next spring we may come back and settle in the city. We'll have to sell everything to be able to rent a place. It is hard these days in the city too, with the war going on and all. The city people don't really like us. They think we're thieves. They even accuse us of stealing children." He laughs. "But the villagers are nicer. It's because, at least in this part of the country, there is a traditional relationship between nomads and villagers."

We reach the city road and are careful to stay well to the side, out of the way of the many trucks and military vehicles. The cars go by with a whoosh and the trucks rumble past with a sound that hurts my eardrums. It's dusty, and all along the road trash and plastic bags are stuck in the low bushes. We rest for a while and drink water from jars. The children eat bread and dates. I decide to stay with the group rather than trying to catch a ride. I don't exactly know why but think it's safer than being alone.

Walking isn't as hard as I thought. My mind is busy deciding where I should go and how I can get any news of Shireen once I'm in the city. Would it be safe to go to the house? I have a feeling it's been confiscated by now or is being watched. It may not even be safe to go and ask some of the neighbors or the man at the newsstand.

We go up and down hill after hill, often stopping to rest where there is a farm, water, or the shade of a tree. Finally, a little after noon, we reach the outskirts of the city. A checkpoint is set up and cars are being stopped. I'm afraid they may recognize me but don't know what I should do, or even what choice I have except to keep walking. I realize I shouldn't feed the fear that is starting within me. For a moment I think I must say something to Davood. But what would I say? With each step I take a deep breath and tell myself to be calm.

"What's going on, Davood?" I ask, nodding toward the group of cars and military men on the road ahead.

"Oh, who knows? Maybe they are searching the cars for opium or draft dodgers." He shakes his head. "Nothing to do with us. They won't bother us. We're used to this. It looks like they're only checking the people leaving the city, not the people going in."

What he says is true, but my fear doesn't go away. I move to his far side to minimize the chance of being seen. Davood seems to realize I'm nervous but doesn't say anything. I walk shoulder to shoulder with him and when we pass the checkpoint, try to move as calmly as possible, not turning my head to look.

When we get closer to the city, Davood explains that they can't go into the city with their animals because the police will give them a hard time. They lead the animals to a field where they can graze on the dried vegetation and be unloaded. Everyone looks exhausted. We drink and eat some bread and dates. After some rest, Davood and one of his sons, with his wife and young daughter, get ready to go to the city. I recognize his wife as the woman who brought us tea last night and see that the tattoo on her chin is a star. The rest of the family will stay with the animals. I say good-bye to those who are staying behind and wave at Abrisham. She waves back, smiling.

Twenty

S HIRAZ IS BUSIER THAN I've ever seen it. Cars and motorcycles
are lined up at gas stations waiting for their ration of gasoline.
On the street that runs to the bazaar, Koranic verses are blasting
out from the loudspeaker of a minaret and vendors are yelling and
shouting to advertise their merchandise—knives and nail clippers,
old watches and radios, nuts and sweets. The Bazaar Vakil, the old
market with its brickwork arches and stretch of shops extending for
more than a mile, is full of people. From their dress I can tell that
most of them have come from nearby towns and villages. I haven't
been inside the bazaar for years. Everything seems the same—the
carpets in geometric and floral patterns and colors of deep red and
blue hung in the carpet shops, the brown and saffron-colored spices
piled on huge round trays, and the cheap shiny fabrics the rural
people like hung up and stacked in piles. There are crowds at all the
shops, looking, examining the merchandise, and bargaining with
the shopkeepers. It gives you the feeling that time has stopped in
this ancient space in the heart of the modern city, where shopkeepers have turned their praying beads and counted their coins the

same way for generations. In the pleasant confusion of the bazaar, I feel safer than on the city streets with *passdars* patrolling.

I tag along with Davood's family as they go from shop to shop, examining everything, admiring everything, asking the price and, after some hesitation, walking away. After a while I realize that I am trying to prolong my time with them so I don't have to be alone and face my fears. I wonder if any of these shopkeepers have heard of the woman who was stoned in the city square. I'm sure any number of them know everything that goes on in this city, but would they be willing to share it with a stranger?

I decide I should be on my way before nightfall and thank Davood for his hospitality and for taking care of Ruzbeh and helping me to get to the city. I tell him that the water pump at the lemon grove has been fixed and that they should come there next fall when there will be a need for fruit pickers. I hate to leave these gentle, calm people who have nothing but their goodness. With a wish for their health and safety, I leave them and make my way through the crowded bazaar.

In the jewelers' section at the end of the bazaar, close to the shrine of Imamzade Shah Cheragh, I search for Musa's brother's shop. If he hasn't left the country and I can find him, maybe he knows something or can gave me a clue what to do. The way news spreads through the bazaar, he must have heard something. Everyone is busy as if there were no war going on. I find the shop, but it's closed. I ask the jeweler next door if the shop will be open.

"No," says the old shopkeeper. "It hasn't been open for a week. I don't know what happened to Ebrahim. He was a good neighbor. There is a rumor that he was arrested"—he brings his head closer—"for spying, but I don't believe that. I think he has left the country to go to Israel. I heard him talking about selling his shop." He looks around to make sure no one is listening. "If this is the way this place is heading, I might start looking to go myself. I have a son in America—in San Jose."

"Ah, San Jose, California?" I ask smiling.

"Yes. Yes. I was there just two years ago and saw the Golden Gate. It was beautiful. The ocean was very nice. There were so many Iranians. A young man like you should try to go. There's no future in this place."

I don't know why he is telling me this, but people love to talk about America if they get a chance.

I thank him and walk away, not knowing where to go or what to do except to lose myself in the narrow winding passages of the bazaar until the noise and the smell of old spices and synthetic perfume start to make my head spin and I rush out to the nearest street.

Soon it will be night and the curfew will be in effect. I'm not afraid, though. I'm determined to do whatever I can to find out about Shireen and avoid anything that will attract attention. I know I've started down a path I must follow no matter the consequences but don't know where to go or whom to ask for information.

There is something strange about the people and the city. The war with its constant flow of casualties and refugees, the threat of nightly air raids, and the ceremonies in the mosques celebrating martyrdom and recruiting people for the front seem to have become an accepted part of life here.

I walk up the street, thinking maybe I should take the risk and go to the house. If I see any sign that it's been confiscated I won't go in. Maybe one of the neighbors could give me some news or the name of a person I could go and see. I try to think of the names of some friends I might be able to look up.

Beside a construction site a group of Afghani workers are gathered. They have finished work for the day and are washing up at a water tap. I consider asking if I can stay with them for the night, knowing that they often stay together in a shack on the site since they don't have their families with them. I start walking toward them when suddenly I remember my friend who has a construction company and hires Afghani workers. Why did it take me so long to think of Javid and his wife, Farideh? When I was hiding in the city those months ago I didn't go to them, thinking it might put them in danger. But now I have to. They've been close friends of Ruzbeh and Shireen's ever since their student days. Like them, they weren't able to finish school when all the universities were closed after the student uprisings, but they kept in touch. Many nights when I came back from America, we would all get together at their place, talking and arguing about the changes in the country and the direction it was heading. Javid was optimistic about the future and Farideh was just the opposite. I can see now that she was right about the pressure that would be put on women's rights as time passed and can remember her saying that women have always been invisible victims in this culture of ours, that they have had to shut up and be quiet, but that they wouldn't stay that way for long and eventually would shout no so loud that the whole world would hear.

I flag down a taxi and tell the driver the name of the neighborhood where Javid and Farideh live. I wonder if they're still in the city or even in the country—so many misfortunes can happen without anyone's knowing. When I get out of the taxi, it takes me a while to get my bearings. I look around for the house. The neighborhood is called Tapeh Televizioun—Television Hill. It's where the Shiraz TV station was built years ago, on the mountainside, and is one of the nicest areas of the city. By the time I find the house and ring the bell, darkness is descending.

A man's voice comes over the intercom. "Ke-eh?"—Who is it?

"Behruz," I say. My voice is dry and shaky. I wait for the click of the automatic door opener but nothing happens, and the same voice comes over the intercom again.

"Who is it?"

"Behruz Pirzad." I speak more loudly this time.

I know I'm at the right place and wonder if they will open the door. They haven't seen or heard from me for more than a year, and if they know what happened to Shireen, they may not want to have anything to do with me.

I am ready to give up and start down the hill when I hear footsteps on the other side of the door and then a long silence.

"Behruz, is it you?"

I recognize Javid's voice this time. "Yes—it's me."

The door opens a crack and I see Javid craning his neck to look down the street before opening the door all the way.

"Come in," he says, "Are you alone?"

He certainly is nervous at seeing me.

"Well." He looks at me as if not recognizing me. "Where've you been all this time, man? Are you okay?"

"Yes. Thank you. Can I talk to you?"

"Sure, come in. Come in."

I enter the familiar courtyard with its wide path and flanking rows of cypress trees. The house sits on a high foundation at the far end of the yard and has wide steps leading up to the entrance. I see someone standing at the top of the stairs. It must be Farideh.

"Hello," I say as I approach her.

She walks down a few steps, smiling, then kisses me and gives me a hug.

"I'm sorry if I've disturbed you."

"No, no. It's just that we haven't heard from you in a long time. Come in, please. Where have you been? You look so thin. We thought for a second you were Ruzbeh. We haven't seen him for months either."

I realize that she doesn't mention Shireen and I don't know how to ask about her. I decide that the best thing is to wait.

When we sit down, Farideh goes out of the room and Javid eyes me in silence. His face looks older and he has less hair than I remember. He seems uneasy, and I imagine he must have many questions on his mind. Farideh comes back with tea and pastries. She has cut her hair short and her neck is bare. She is dressed nicely, wearing a silver necklace and turquoise earrings. I realize it's been a long time since I've seen a woman's bare neck.

"I'm sorry," I say. "Were you about to go out?"

"Oh, no," she says. "We were at Javid's sister's this afternoon and just got back."

"I'm glad I found you at home."

She holds the tray out to me. From the look in her eyes, I can guess what is in her mind. She must blame me for what happened to Shireen and wonder how I could have started a relationship with my own brother's wife. I take a cup of tea and she puts the tray on the table and sits down.

I remember how night after night we discussed the political situation and the Americans being held hostage at the embassy, an action that branded Iran as an uncivilized country, isolated us, and damaged our credibility and culture and is something we may never recover from. Javid saw it as a way to fight the imperialist West, a view of many Iranian leftists at the time. We argued about imperialism, Western democracy and human rights, and the events that were taking our country in the wrong direction. We talked about the separation of religion and state, and how when a society gives the first priority to God, then naturally the next priority will go to those who represent God, and so on and on, with the ordinary citizens coming last, if not left out altogether.

Farideh and Shireen talked about their early student activities and described the day they had gone to Tehran for the International Women's Day march that more than a million people participated in, but still the women lost. Both Shireen and Farideh believed that the government would hold on to power for years to come, and Javid would disagree saying that the Islamists didn't have the sophistication to run the country. I thought that there was no need for sophistication—that ignoring human rights didn't require sophistication. Shireen and Farideh were mostly on my side, and I enjoyed that.

It was interesting to see Shireen at a gathering, how quick she was to express her views in sign language. We had all picked up some of the language by that time. Farideh and Shireen would often have their own conversation going on, with Ruzbeh keeping quiet and listening. After we had worn ourselves out talking, Javid, who loved classical Persian music, would play his oud, and the low and sad strains of the lute and his deep voice would take us away from the disturbing events of the day.

I look at Javid and Farideh and wonder what they are thinking. It seems we are all avoiding something—or maybe just don't know where to start.

We drink our tea in a silence that seems to last hours. Finally Javid says, "Well, where have you been? Where is Ruzbeh?"

"I was at the lemon grove. As for Ruzbeh, I saw him only briefly yesterday after many months. He's back there now and I hope that he will stay there and not go back to wandering the desert."

There is another long silence. Then, eyeing me, Farideh says, "If no one wants to say anything, let me start."

She is bold and direct, as always. "Behruz, we were looking for you. Everything came to us secondhand. First we heard you were killed, then that you had run away and been captured. We didn't believe you were captured, because we know people who would have told us. We had no idea where to look for you or Ruzbeh. We went to your house. It was guarded. We went to the Naranjestan. We hadn't been there for years. It looked abandoned and there was no sign that anyone had been there . . ."

I interrupt her. "What happened to Shireen? Do you know?"

They look at each other.

"That's why I'm here," I say firmly. "If you know, you must tell me. If you don't know, I need to leave." I get up.

"Take it easy, Behruz," Javid says. "Sit down please." I can hear the pleading in his voice but don't sit down.

"She's saved," Farideh says finally, her voice breaking.

"Saved?" My eyes go back and forth between them.

"Yes—saved," Javid says.

"Then what I've heard is true. Where is she? Tell me, please."

"Calm down," Farideh says, wiping her eyes.

Javid puts his hand on her shoulder. I sit down, leaning toward them.

"She's not here," Farideh says.

"Then tell me, for God's sake. Is she in jail?"

"No. She's out of the country."

I stare at her. Then at Javid.

"Out of the country? I don't understand."

She gives me a sharp look to indicate I should keep calm and listen.

"Yes—she's gone to Afghanistan."

"Afghanistan!?"

"Yes, and she's safe where she is."

"Please," I plead. "I don't understand. Why Afghanistan?"

"It is complicated and difficult—she was saved and not saved," Farideh says, on the verge of crying.

"Farideh-*joon*," Javid says. "Be calm, dear."

I feel frustrated and angry that they don't just spell it out.

At last Farideh continues. "She managed to pull herself free." Her voice chokes. "The woman who was in charge of her in prison—or wherever it was they were holding her—a few days beforehand told her that the only way to survive was to manage to free herself, that she shouldn't panic or be afraid, that she should dig herself out no matter what. And if she did, according to Islamic law, the stoning would stop because she would be considered innocent.

"The woman wouldn't even tell us her name. She had told Shireen that she would take her to her family. Shireen had written down our address."

Farideh grows quiet. I close my eyes, not knowing what to say. I search for words, but everything that comes to mind seems hollow and absurd. I wait and Farideh goes on. "She was in shock, frightened and broken. Her hands and fingers were cut and her face . . ."

She gets up and leaves the room. I feel a lump in my throat and struggle to fight back the tears and keep from breaking down in front of them.

I hear Javid's voice as if from far away. "Behruz, are you all right? Do you want to lie down?"

"No. Just tell me. Tell me what happened, Javid."

He takes his time taking a sip from his tea as if he does not wish to talk and then says, "It was dark when the woman rang the bell and brought her to us. We called a doctor who is a friend of ours. He came over right away. It was almost two months before she started to show signs of recovery. It wasn't physical, you see. Yes she had cuts and bruises, but it was the mental shock. I guess none of us could imagine what it was like. Farideh took care of her, even though she was ill the whole time. I played the oud for them every night. I would sit next to Shireen's bed and play. Farideh slept in the same room and wouldn't leave her by herself."

Farideh comes in and sits beside Javid. She has washed her face but her eyes are red.

"Are you all right?" Javid asks her.

She nods.

I feel awful. "I'm sorry, Farideh," I say.

"We looked for you and Ruzbeh," Javid goes on. "We looked everywhere. We knew Ruzbeh was gone—that he had run away or disappeared somewhere. We went to the lemon grove again and didn't see anyone. Shireen told us your mother and hers were in the village, but she didn't want us to go to them. She couldn't bear it. So we didn't. We thought you would come around if you hadn't been captured. What happened to you? We heard you were killed trying to run away."

I get up and walk to the window. How foolish I have been. I let self-pity overwhelm me and eat away at the courage that I needed all those months. I let fear keep me around that barren lemon grove. Why didn't I think of Javid and Farideh all that time? I could have come here then. Maybe I could have helped Shireen somehow. Maybe I could have figured out a way.

"Tell me what happened to her. Why is she in Afghanistan?"

"Because she had nobody here. Because we had no other choice!" Farideh snaps at me. "Where were you? How could you leave her and now come asking for her?"

I look at Javid. He sees my pleading look and turns to Farideh. "Take it easy, *azizam.*"

"We couldn't find you," Javid says. "And the woman who brought Shireen came back later and said we should send her somewhere safe, away from here if possible, because the religious judge who gave the sentence was questioning how she came to be freed. He thought there must have been a conspiracy or bribery at work for her to have been able to escape."

"We didn't know what to believe," Javid continues. "Was this woman telling the truth? We didn't know. Anything is possible in this place. We thought she wanted a reward for bringing her to us, and we had already responded generously. There is so much contradiction and irrationality these days that you lose your sense of normalcy. Every few days we took her from one friend's house to another, and finally, when she was better, we helped her leave the country."

"Why out of the country? You could have . . ."

"Could have what?" Farideh says, raising her voice. "Shireen wanted to go." She turns to Javid. "Didn't she, Javid?"

"How could that be?"

"Take it easy, Behruz," says Javid. "You look ill. You need to rest."

"How is it possible?"

"We really had no choice," Farideh says. "She wanted to go—certainly you should understand that. After what happened it was as if nothing mattered to her anymore. There was nothing left for her to hang on to. The house had been confiscated, or was in the process of being confiscated. She and Ruzbeh had become estranged, and you . . . well, I don't know what to say."

She pauses for a moment. "She had only one thought left, to rescue herself. And she intended to live no matter what. Also, I personally would have done anything so that they couldn't get their hands on her again. She was even afraid to go to her own mother. Besides, it would have broken her mother's heart to see her in that condition."

Javid puts his hand on Farideh's shoulder again and she continues with bitterness in her voice. "How could a woman raise her head in this city after what happened? She couldn't have gone anywhere without being eyed and pointed at like . . . like the woman in *The Scarlet Letter*. That was fiction but here it's real. And it's happening all over the country. With no sign of stopping, and none of us is doing anything about it . . ."

She stops talking, gets up, and leaves the room. Javid follows her. I sink down in the sofa, thinking that I don't possess an ounce of the insight and courage of either Farideh or Shireen. At the worst possible time, Shireen tried to save herself, while I did the opposite. And have I ever gone out of my way to help anyone the way so many people have tried to help me? I resolve to change, to do things differently.

Night has fallen and from the window I can see the flickering lights of the city down in the valley. All at once the room goes dark. It takes me a moment to realize that the power is out and the whole city is drowned in darkness. It seems like a long time before Javid comes in with a portable propane lamp. Our shadows, fat and surreal, are cast on the walls and the ceiling.

"Here we go again," Javid says. "God knows, but it may be a few hours before we will have the electricity back. This has been happening often these days."

Farideh comes in with a glass of water in her hand.

"I'm sorry, Farideh," I say softly. "I'm causing you such anxiety, but why Afghanistan? Another country engulfed in chaos and war."

"Well," Javid says after a while, "it's the safest avenue we knew, and we had done it before. We managed to send a few friends out of the country through Afghanistan and Pakistan, and from there with the help of the United Nations they were able to go to Europe and Canada and even the United States—friends who were in the opposition and in danger, also a Baha'i family who were our neighbors when we lived in the Golestan area. They were chased out of their house after the revolution and had to live in hiding. If Shireen gets to the U.N. office in Pakistan, she'll have no problem getting to the West. She has a strong case."

"Yes," Farideh says. "It was the safest way we knew."

"I have many Afghans who work for me," Javid goes on. "Every few months they go back to see their families and sometimes they take their families back and forth. We sent Shireen out dressed as an Afghani woman with a man we trust. She's with his family in Kandahar."

I get up and go to the window to look out at the dark city. "You must help me," I say. "I need to go there. I need to go and find her. Javid, can you help me? I need to go to her."

Farideh, as if she has been waiting for my words, turns to Javid. "We could send him with Zamirvali. The same way."

"Things are not as they were a few months ago," Javid says after some thought. "It may not be as easy, but I'll look into it. There would be some paperwork to be done, and it might take a couple of weeks." He turns to me. "Are you sure you are up to this? You look ill."

"I'll be fine after a few days' rest. Who is Zamirvali?"

"He's an Afghan," Javid says. "A trusted friend who works for me. He took Shireen to Afghanistan. I need to talk to him, but we would need to be careful and not let anyone know you're here."

"Our plan was that Shireen would go to Pakistan from there," Farideh says. "It may not be as easy as we think for a woman by herself. If you were with her it would be much easier to make it to the U.N. refugee office at the border with Pakistan."

I feel weak and think I'm going to pass out. I know my illness is starting to come back. I tell them that I need to lie down.

Javid brings me some aspirin, then takes the lamp and helps me to the guest bedroom. He pulls back the blankets and I lie down on the bed. When he leaves, taking the lamp with him, the room is pitch-black . . . I close my eyes and see a figure in the distance. I see the flare of her red dress and her hair flying in the wind. She is waving, but in greeting or farewell? For a moment I think she is calling for help. Webs of light and dust break my vision. She moves away and fades from view. I must run to her, run into the desert. I want to call after her but can't open my mouth.

Twenty-one

I T'S DARK AND I WAKE UP breathing hard, coughing and sweating and not knowing where I am. I hear muffled voices in the other room and it takes me a few seconds to realize I'm at Javid's. The door opens and Javid stands there, the hallway light pouring past him into the room.

"Good you're awake," he says. "I was waiting for you to wake up. We've called someone to come over. He's a doctor and a trusted friend. You need to be looked at."

"No I don't. I'm okay."

"You do need to be looked at. Anyway, he's here."

I have neither the patience nor the will to fight Javid. He comes back with the doctor and turns the light on. I close my eyes for a moment and, when I open them, an Indian doctor with extremely white teeth is smiling at me.

"I'm Dr. Suresh Sharma."

"Hello," I say, shaking his extended hand.

He starts to examine me, looking under my eyelids, in my ears and throat, taking my pulse, and listening to my heart and my breathing.

"Javid tells me you were in America," he says in English.

I nod.

"Where?"

"The Midwest."

"Chicago?"

"Near there." I don't really feel like talking or going into detail. I'm afraid that if he finds out how sick I am it will jeopardize my chance of getting to Afghanistan.

"I would love very much to go to America," he says, sighing. "It's not good here anymore, or even safe. Sorry to say this, but it's true." He shakes his head from side to side as if it's loose on his neck. "The Namazi Hospital here was the best in the Middle East, and I worked with good Iranian and American doctors. They're all gone now— not just the Americans, the Iranians too. Everything has stopped. There is zero research done. No medicine. No equipment. We're overwhelmed by the war casualties."

He puts his stethoscope on again. When it touches my back, I jump at its cold feel. He tells me to breathe deeply and moves it around listening to my lungs.

"I'm working on going to America to become a surgeon," he says, taking the stethoscope out of his ears. "I came here almost ten yeas ago—in the good old days, as they say now." He smiles. "And now I'm stuck here because of circumstances. Circumstances—we are all here or anywhere because of circumstances. You in America, then here. Me in Hyderabad, now here! Tomorrow who knows? Even the gods are in our lives because of circumstances."

He pushes on my kidneys and I cry out. With a frown he eases his touch and goes on with the examination.

"Your kidneys are sensitive. Do you urinate a lot?"

I hesitate at first, but then I answer him. "It seems that I do."

He tells me to lie on my back and pushes down on my chest and the lower part of my belly. I feel a sharp pain, but this time control myself. I don't say a word about the incident in the Naranjestan. I'm afraid he is going to tell me that I'm seriously ill.

"It seems that your lungs are weak. Do you smoke?"

"No."

"Possibly it's from being in the countryside—in all that dust and wind. You have a temperature and your blood pressure is low. I would like to take urine and blood samples and do some tests, but you would need to come to the hospital for that. I suggest that you get some rest. I'll write prescriptions for something that will make you sleep better and something for your kidneys. Unfortunately there are not many good medicines available now, but these will do the job. And above all you need to rest—rest as a sitting Buddha rests." He gives me a wide smile.

I thank him and tell him I hope he makes it to America. He gives Javid the prescription.

"Get these pills for him and have him rest. Get him a damp towel to put on his forehead. I would love to stay and chat," he says as he prepares to leave, "but it's late."

Javid walks out with him and comes back in a few minutes. "How did you like our doctor friend?" he says. "He never runs out of things to say, especially about himself or India."

I force a smile.

"Well, as the good Dr. Sharma said, you need to rest. The drug-stores are closed at this hour. I'll get the medicine for you tomorrow. Let's hope I can find one that carries them."

Twenty-two

I N THE PAST TWO WEEKS, away from the open country, I have
been able to relax a bit by reading poetry and preparing my mind
for the journey. Afternoons I sit in Farideh's flower garden inside the
walled courtyard. It's a large courtyard, much larger than those in
most houses here, and a place to enjoy. Farideh works in the garden
almost every afternoon for an hour or so after she comes home from
her work at city hall.

Her garden isn't like traditional Persian courtyard gardens that
have a *hoze*—pool—in the middle, surrounded by symmetric plots
laid out in a geometric design like a Persian carpet. At first glance
it's a riot of colors and shapes that look mismatched, as if Jackson
Pollock had stood on the redbrick edging of the garden and madly
splashed his colors down. But when you stand gazing at the rich
textures of red and yellow, green and white, orange and purple, you
realize that it's designed to put you into an abstract space alive with
order, balance, and rhythm. After a while you see how everything—
the spaces, shapes, colors, and fragrances—comes together and takes

you away from the chaos of this old city that was once famous for its wine and rose gardens.

Farideh says that in any part of this ancient country there are stories that show how gardens and poetry have been complementing each other throughout the ages. One that she says she enjoys the most is about a poet-king who loved gardens. He built a garden with a small stream snaking through and filled the garden with flowering plants from different parts of the country. The king would invite poets to the garden and have them spread out at equal intervals alongside the stream. Cups of wine with gold coins in the bottom and balanced on leaves would be floated down the water. The challenge was that the first poet would recite the first line of a poem and the next poet had to compose the second line by the time a cup of wine reached him and so on. Any poet who couldn't make the next rhyme would lose his chance of grabbing the passing cup.

How we would be content now with a forbidden glass of red wine.

"You must be able to find wine around here," I say after she tells me the story.

"Yes," she answers. "Practically every basement in the city has become a winery. But you have to consider the consequences of every act in this city of ours."

I think she is refraining from saying that I had acted foolishly in the past. She drinks her tea and tells me that three things have kept them going—the garden, Javid's music, and reading. "Can you believe it?" she says, "Javid and I are not even thirty, yet we live like old people. And we're the lucky ones." Then she stops. "You know, I miss Shireen so much. I don't have very many friends here anymore. Most of them have left. We worked in the garden together—she loved it." She reflects for a moment. "It was like therapy for her. She would plant and I would water. We worked for hours in the summer heat. Shireen planted most of the *gole-laleh abaassi* and *gole-laadan*—four o'clocks and nasturtiums. She had a way of doing things. Just look at those flowers, how they complement one another."

I look at the pink trumpets of the four o'clocks and the gold and orange nasturtiums sprawling along the pathway and wish she were here to see them.

"You know, Behruz, I love children. So does Javid. We wanted to have a child, but we've decided not to, at least for now, not while we have to live with this war that seems to have no end. If it works out and we get to a more civilized place, maybe then. Like Javid told you the other night, we're serious about leaving. Many of our friends have applied to go to Canada. Some have gone to Europe, some to America."

I am surprised at the way Farideh has opened up to me. Being in the garden seems to have relaxed her and made her talk freely. I listen, feeling sorry and confused about what the future could be in a place where the younger generation is deprived of an ordinary way of life.

Talking to Javid these past few nights, I have realized that he has started to be much more relaxed with me. In the past I had sensed his jealousy. I guess he thought of Ruzbeh and me as spoiled children with money and land, and to a degree resented my having had the opportunity to go to America while he had to work from childhood and was forced to depend only on himself. He was a good student and passed the university entrance exams to study architecture only to be unable to finish just one semester short of graduating because the universities had been closed. At the time, he had Marxist ideas and argued passionately in favor of the abolition of private property. Now he's wealthy because of his own efforts and insight. He made his money by buying confiscated properties and the fancy cars and Persian carpets that were left behind by wealthy military officers, government officials, and university heads who had fled the country or been executed or jailed. This house is impressive and stylish with stone stairs and columns at the entrance replicating those at Persepolis. The spacious living room has huge windows that open to the city below. The fireplace is flanked by two guards like those in the ruins of the ancient palace. I can't help wondering about who owned it and where the family is, or whether they're even alive.

The other day on the afternoon news I saw an interview with

several Afghani men talking about the war and consequent problems in Afghanistan. I got upset and told Javid they shouldn't have sent Shireen there. "Listen, Behruz," he said, "don't you get it, man? Don't you see what is happening here? There are no choices. If you find a way, you're lucky. Do you know how many people are running for their lives, going on foot across the desert to Afghanistan and Pakistan or over the mountains of Kurdistan to Turkey? Many are robbed and cheated if not abandoned by the smugglers. But then, why should you get it? You're so disillusioned that nothing seems to reach you. Sorry Behruz, but these are the facts. Anyone who has a chance is getting out. The smart ones are those who got out years ago and stayed out." I noticed his sarcastic smile and knew he was thinking of me. "Everything is changing for the worse here. What happened to Shireen wasn't an isolated incident—that sort of barbarism is happening all over the country. She's lucky she is out. That's the only way we could help her."

I kept quiet, not wanting to say anything more. In the evening, after a good dinner of the sort I hadn't had for many months, Javid played his lute and sang in his deep, sad voice that sounded even sadder than I remembered.

> Oh, love, all the best years of my youth
> I searched for you
> up the mountains, down the valleys,
> in the crooked city streets.

> The desert made me thirsty
> The forest made me sleepy
> The city choked me
> But your love in my heart
> Kept me alive.

The Indian doctor has come twice to see me. God how he talked, first trying to persuade me to go to the hospital for tests, then telling me about his plans to leave the country. He has managed to get an acceptance letter from a medical school in Milwaukee. A friend who works there sent it to him. He said he doesn't even know what the place is like, but it's a start and if he doesn't like it there he'll go somewhere else.

"I can't stand the aristocratic behavior of the British," he explained. "Otherwise I would go to England. I think America is a better choice. It's like India, with many different kinds of people and religions. Of course if only we could get people to have fewer children, maybe India would have a better future too."

His plan was to go to Mumbai to apply for a visa to the United States and see his mother as well. If I ever go back to America, he says, I should look him up.

"And don't get me wrong about leaving Shiraz," he went on. "I love the city and the climate, but all my Iranian colleagues have left or are leaving, and I'm seeing things happening here that dishearten a believer in nonviolence. What have we humans learned from history after all? Shouldn't we learn from past mistakes? Why does history always repeat itself? Or should I say do we let history repeat itself. Pardon me for going on like this."

Before I can leave for Afghanistan, I need to be sure about two things. One is that Ruzbeh will stay with Farideh and Javid as they suggested, and the other that they will bring Mother to the city, since she needs medical attention. Javid has promised to follow up and find out what has happened to our house—it belongs to Mother and she should be able to get it back.

Last week, Javid and Farideh went to the Naranjestan to bring Ruzbeh to the city and try their best to let him know that Shireen has left the country, without giving too much detail. To their surprise, he took the news better than we had feared, but he decided to stay with Mother and come to the city later.

Today Farideh left work early and went to the village to try to find Ruzbeh. I want him here so he can be seen by the doctor and get the medicine he needs. I know Farideh has a sweet way with him and will be able to convince him to come. I wish Javid could have gone with her, but there were some complications at city hall about one of the apartment buildings he is constructing.

It's late afternoon and Farideh should be back by now. I wonder whether something has gone wrong. Has Ruzbeh run away again and is she looking for him? I've been trying to be more positive the past two weeks, thinking that soon I'll be leaving and I don't want anything to go wrong or make me lose confidence.

In the garden, as sunset approaches, the dark flowers are fading and the white ones are coming into sharp relief. I'm engaged in watching the slow change of the colors when I hear the door and Javid walks in, briefcase in hand.

"I didn't see Farideh's car," he says in an agitated tone. "Isn't she back yet?"

"No," I say. "I've been waiting."

"God, what a day," he says. "There's no logic in the head of any person in the city hall." Then after a moment he adds, "I hope Farideh is not in trouble."

"Why? What happened?"

"There are roadblocks at all the major intersections and cars are being checked. It wasn't a good day to send her for Ruzbeh. What a stupid mistake to let her go by herself."

"Do you think something happened, Javid?"

"What if they stopped her with Ruzbeh in a private car? She could be in trouble, being with a man she's not married or related to."

"Oh jeez," I exclaim and see Javid staring at me. I realize this expression, so common in America, must sound strange to his ears.

"Maybe we should go after her, Javid."

"Yes, we ought to," he says.

I walk with him through the courtyard to the main door, wondering if this is another situation where I'm going to lose my nerve.

"Wait a minute," Javid says. "I don't think it's a good idea for you to come. What if we are stopped at a roadblock and you are recognized."

At that moment we hear a car pull up. Javid opens the door halfway. "It's Farideh," he says and opens the gate for her to drive in.

Farideh gets out of the car, followed by Musa and Ruzbeh. I'm relieved to see them but surprised that Musa has come.

Farideh winks and whispers to me as she passes, "Here, I brought your brother. It wasn't easy, but here he is, as handsome as ever." I want to hug her, but I can only manage to say thank you.

"Hello, young man." It's Musa coming to shake my hand. I smile and remember how he calls me young man. "Don't you know it's not polite to leave without saying good-bye?" He smiles and looks happy to see me. "We've been having quite a time at the orchard!"

Ruzbeh looks tired and seems nervous.

"Salaam, Ruzbeh," I say as I embrace and kiss him. I realize right away that he is much better than he was the afternoon in the Naranjestan when I left him. I'm sure Musa has taken care of him and made him rest. I step back and look at him, his hair cut and face clean-shaven, and the sports coat he has on. If you didn't know him—well, you would never guess anything was wrong.

Javid shakes hands with Musa and then hugs and kisses Ruzbeh. "It's been a long time, my friend. I'm glad to see you. Let's go in."

At the moment we turn to go back to the house we hear a motorcycle pull up.

"Oh," Musa says, "Kemal is here."

Javid opens the door, and Kemal pushes his motorcycle into the yard. He shakes hands with everyone and looks at me as if he were seeing me for the first time.

We go in and Javid brings a tray with cups of tea. Farideh comes into the living room. She has taken off her scarf and chador. "It took a long time," she says. I sense disturbance in her manner and wonder if something is wrong. "Musa and Kemal decided to come, and I spent some time with your mother and Bibi Khanom. They seemed fine. Your mother says she's ready to come back to the city."

Ruzbeh is quiet. I wish we were alone so we could talk. I ask about the Naranjestan.

"Things are fine," Musa says. "Everything is going smoothly. Things have been going well since the day the pump started to work."

He sits back in his chair and, looking at me, launches into a story.

"That afternoon when I saw you sitting under the willow tree where you always sit, I called out, 'Behruz, come and wash yourself—we're going to have tea—we're going to have a celebration for the water coming back,' but you didn't move."

"You were calling Behruz!" Ruzbeh says, smiling as he finishes his tea.

"How would I have known, young man?" Musa replies. "Then I walked over to get you to come and join us."

"Yes, you did," Ruzbeh says laughing. "You looked right at me and said, 'Behruz, don't you want to come and have some tea?'"

My heart fills with joy seeing him like this, but at the same time I feel anxious, knowing that his behavior could change at any moment.

"Later I was preparing my water pipe and you told me that the Gypsies were going south. I stopped and looked up. 'Gypsies? What is he saying?' It was then that I realized I was talking to Ruzbeh. I was taken aback, I can tell you."

Javid and Farideh watch Musa with interest. I can see they are fascinated by him.

"How could this be?" Musa continues after taking a sip of tea. "Behruz was here all along and now suddenly it's Ruzbeh here beside me. Is this a vision? Have these young men been playing with me all along, switching back and forth all summer and I didn't know it? Has Kemal got something to do with this? Then I yelled for Kemal to come over."

"I rushed out," Kemal says, "thinking something had happened to the children and saw Musa pointing at Ruzbeh. 'What's the matter, old man?' I said as I went up to Ruzbeh and, shaking hands with him, said that it was a very good day to come back. The day the pump is fixed."

"How did you know it was Ruzbeh?" Javid asks.

"I'm not sure but I knew right away."

Farideh bursts into a laugh. "I wish I'd been there."

We have a simple dinner that Farideh and Javid have prepared. When they take the dishes to the kitchen, I hear them arguing and a moment later Javid rushes into the living room.

"I wish someone had told me about the roadblock." He looks at Musa and Kemal.

"Well, young man," Musa says, "it was over as soon as it started and we didn't want to spoil the evening. Things are difficult enough as they are."

In confusion I look at them.

"They were stopped at a roadblock and questioned," Javid explains. "It was at the entrance to the city. This could be a big problem."

"I was telling Javid," Farideh says, coming back into the room, "that the person who questioned us looked familiar. I think he was at the university when we were there and belonged to the radical Islamists. He always caused problems for the girls who weren't wearing scarves. After the revolution he joined a militia. I don't know if he recognized me. Kemal talked to him and he let us go. Now Javid is all upset."

Kemal breaks in. "I don't think there's any problem. I know some of those guys. I told him we worked at Mrs. Farideh Rahimi's farm and were going to the city to buy some equipment for a broken tractor. Looking me up and down, the guard said, 'We need farmers like you these days! We need to grow what we need and become self-sufficient so we can put an end to importing goods.'" A self-assured look covers Kemal's face. "That's what he said, and here we are."

"I don't trust any of these people," Javid says. "They could have followed you. And if they come here . . ." He hesitates. "We need to come up with something."

I wouldn't blame him for getting rid of me right on the spot, I think to myself. They have already risked so much.

"Well," Javid says, "I better take them to my sister's. That would be the best, I think. She's out of town. The house isn't that far and the curfew hasn't started yet. I'll take you all there now, and early in the morning I'll come and take Behruz and Zamirvali to the bus station."

Everybody gets up quickly as if the guards were actually on their way to the house.

Twenty-three

THE MORNING IS BREAKING, and the sound of the muezzins travels up the hill from the city below. Musa comes to wake me up, but I've been awake for a while. I have my Afghani clothes on and have been anxiously waiting.

It's cold this time of year and seems the worst time for a journey—a long journey across the desert and jagged mountains of two ancient countries. I insisted on leaving for Afghanistan as soon as possible. Now everything is arranged and I'm ready. Javid managed to get me an Afghani identity card from the labor department—it had belonged to a man named Valid Shah, who died in an accident at a brick factory where he worked. Javid wouldn't say how much he had to pay as a bribe to get it.

Last night under darkness we managed to get to Javid's sister with no problem, although the whole event added to my anxiety. I was sure something would go wrong and prevent me from leaving for Afghanistan.

I'm pleased beyond measure that Ruzbeh is here. It would have been very hard not to see him before going away. He said he has been staying with Mother and been taking his medicine. Also it's obvious that spending time with Musa has been very positive for him. At Javid's I watched him closely to see if I could detect any signs of uneasiness. He was calm and quiet. I've seen him this way many times but know that his silence can lead to a deep depression that pushes him to leave and wander the streets.

Last night at last I got a chance to be alone with Ruzbeh and wanted to ask what was on his mind, but I was afraid how he would react. I didn't want to throw him off balance, so I carefully asked about Mother and the Naranjestan before bringing the conversation around to us. I knew I might not have another chance to talk to him or even see him again.

"Ruzbeh," I said nervously, "you must hate me."

He stared at me in a such a serious way that I hated myself for asking the question and prayed he wouldn't be upset.

"No, I don't hate you," he said.

"I'm glad," I said. "I want to tell you that I'll do everything possible to find Shireen. Maybe then you can come and join us."

"Find her first," he said firmly.

I looked at him, trying not to get emotional. I didn't want him to lose the confidence he had been showing.

"*Hatman, hatman*—of course, of course. I must," I told him. "And I want you to promise me you'll stay with Farideh and Javid."

I got up and hugged him. "You'll stay with them?"

"Yes," he said. "I'll try." We looked at each other close to tears. I felt that I had just raised my head above water and taken a deep breath.

"I would have liked to take you with me," I said, "but Javid didn't want to send both of us together since the chance of succeeding would be lower."

"You go find her first," he repeated.

Musa, Kemal, and Ruzbeh are in the dining room, and when I walk in, all three stop eating and stare at me.

"Behruz, you amaze me," Musa says. "I had no idea. You look just like an Afghan. I'm sure it will make it safer for you and everything will go fine."

"I'm not amazed," Kemal says, laughing and looking at my turban and baggy pants. "Like we say, if there were water, he would be a professional swimmer!"

I ignore him and look at Ruzbeh, who is feeling the material of my shirt.

"Looks good on you," he says smiling.

I return his smile and take a cup of tea but don't really feel like drinking or eating anything. At that moment we hear the door and Javid and Farideh walk in.

"Wow," Javid says. "Very nice!"

Farideh touches my shoulder and smiles. "You look handsome," she says. "Watch out for the Kandahari girls when you get there."

I smile back at her. I know they are all as nervous as I am and are trying hard to be supportive.

"We'd better get going," Javid says. "We need to stop on the way and pick up Zamirvali at the construction site."

Farideh hands me two books of poetry. "The *Rubaiyat* is for you, and Farrokhzad's *Another Birth* is for Shireen." Her eyes are moist. "She liked to borrow it when she was here."

Musa has a small plastic bag. "Kemal and I got you this. It's dried fruits and nuts to take on the bus."

I thank them and put everything in my shoulder bag. When we are in the yard, Musa holds up a Koran for me to kiss and walk under.

"Come on, Musa," Kemal says, "you can't believe in this."

"Hush, Kemal," Musa says.

I go along with these rituals and am even more surprised when Farideh pours water on the ground behind me, a Persian custom I don't even know the meaning of.

"Young man," Musa says as he gives me a hug, "take care of yourself, you hear?"

Kemal shakes my hand calmly. "Don't worry about Ruzbeh, your mother, or the Naranjestan. I'll take care of things here. Remember that Kemal is a man of his word."

Farideh hugs me. "Find Shireen. Don't worry about us. I'll do all I can for your mother and will send Ruzbeh to you when the time is right. Be strong. Be hopeful."

I become aware of Ruzbeh standing close beside me. We embrace and everyone is quiet. It seems that neither of us wants to let go. I hold him tighter and can feel his anxiety. Finally we step back and wipe our tears. He puts a small box in my shoulder bag. "Give this to Shireen," he says, trying to keep back his tears.

At the moment I'm ready to get into the car, I ask Javid if Ruzbeh could come to the bus station with us.

"Sure," he says. "Let's hurry."

Ruzbeh gets in and sits next to me. I'm pleased that I will have a few more minutes with him. As we drive away, I turn and see them standing by the door waving.

Good-bye, Farideh, I say to myself. You, too, be strong and hopeful and try to make it out of Iran. Good-bye, old man. Good-bye, dear friend—how you softened my pain with your kindness. Good-bye, Kemal. Be good to the old man. Be good and learn from him.

Twenty-four

AFGHANS WITH BUNDLES OF CLOTHES and food fill the bus. It surprises me that there are women and children among them—I thought it was only the men who came to work or escape the war. With my turban and baggy pants, I look like any Afghani man in the crowd. I even have dark-red *tasbih,* the prayer beads that all the men carry. Here in the back of the bus I sit beside Zamirvali, a man in his forties who looks like he has been in the sun every day of his life. He sits quietly but notices everything around him. He is whispering a prayer and turning his prayer beads between his rough fingers. I sit quietly while turning mine.

Last week I worked a few hours a day alongside Zamirvali and his Afghani coworkers, carrying bricks and shoveling dirt so that my hands would look like those of a worker. I let my beard grow and learned how to roll a turban and keep it on my head. Zamirvali is helping me to mimic the speech of the Afghans, who speak Persian with a distinctive accent that sounds archaic and humorous to an Iranian ear. We have an agreement that if we run into a problem with the authorities, we've never met and don't know each other.

It took us a day and a half on the desert roads, cold at night and hot during the day, to get to the city of Zahedan, the capital of the Iranian province of Baluchistan. All through the trip, we passed roadblocks one after another. I was nervous each time I had to show my ID card and hadn't totally calmed down when we would be stopped again. Many times we had to get off the bus so it could be searched for weapons or whatever contraband the Kalashnikov-carrying guards were looking for.

Each small town we passed looked like the previous one—dusty, with rows of green and black banners, portraits of war martyrs posted along main streets that were almost all named Khayban Imam Khomeini, and Koranic verses blasting from mosques. All the gas stations had long lines of vehicles waiting for gas and people crowded by the pumps. At the roadside teahouses and bus stops, there were children in old clothes, some barefoot and some wearing plastic sandals that let their toes peek out. At a few places the children were begging and washing car windows for money.

We rested at Zahedan for a few hours and changed buses. The teahouses were full of Baluchi men. Almost all the Baluchis had huge mustaches and rode big motorcycles. Zamirvali told me the motorcycle is the ultimate vehicle for smuggling opium, guns, and sometimes people through the desert and across the border.

From Zahedan it took half a day to get to the city of Zabol, close to the border with Afghanistan, and from there it was a short ride to the border crossing. I was afraid they would search me and worried about the dollar bills that Javid had given me just before I left. I was carrying them in a flat sack under my shirt and had my forged documents in my pocket ready to show when asked for. The crossing was crowded with Afghans, Baluchis, and Pakistanis taking merchandise across. I was surprised to see a group of Yemeni Arabs, who said proudly that they were going to Afghanistan to fight the Russians. Because the border crossing had been closed for two days—it was anyone's guess as to why—a disorganized row of buses, minibuses, and trucks stretched out on each side, the constant wind and blowing sand adding to the chaotic situation. The bribery was as open as the desert.

We passed the border into Afghanistan with no problem. The

countryside seemed deserted compared to Iran. Zamirvali said that the Zabol border crossing was the safest one. The border guards know that the opium smugglers don't go through there but instead pick the hardest and most impassable routes over the mountains, places even the military people think twice about using.

Since yesterday when we passed the border, I've been feeling sick and not sleeping well. It's cold, and the bus isn't in good shape. The wind howls and blows in through every window. The shaking rattles my bones and my mind wavers at the edge of consciousness. I ask Zamirvali for water to wet my mouth but after drinking the salty water, feel thirstier. He gives me some dried apricots, saying it will help my thirst. We have oranges we bought from roadside vendors just outside Shiraz that I eat when I'm thirsty.

Zamirvali turns his prayer beads and watches the countryside through the dusty windows of the bus as if he doesn't want to miss a hill or a village. I can tell from his reserved conduct that he's been through a lot. I like it that he doesn't talk unless it's necessary, since I don't have the energy for conversation.

"We are entering Lashkar Gah territory," he says as we go down a mountainside. I notice that his voice shakes and he speaks haltingly. He wipes his face with his handkerchief.

"There," he says, pointing to a hill in the distance. "My village used to be behind that hill. The people have all gone to Pakistan and Iran. My family still has land there, but there are mines everywhere and no one lives there. One of my brothers was killed fighting the Russians and one went to Pakistan with his family. I never thought a village could die like that. Life is full of surprises, isn't it?" He shakes his head.

"One day I was a farmer with my own land, now I'm a laborer in another country. We never know what's coming our way, what's awaiting us on the other side of the hill. Only Allah knows. We are all in his hands." He pauses for a minute.

"I had to take my family to Kandahar. My plan was to take them with me to Iran, but then the war with Iraq started, as if we didn't have enough problems. Can you believe that? We ran away from the war here only to face it there."

Not many cars are on the roads except for military Jeeps and small trucks carrying armed and bearded men. Yesterday we couldn't travel because there was combat on the mountain road ahead of us. We saw a group of mujahedin carrying weapons up the mountain on donkeys and could hear the sound of bombs falling. When the Russian MiGs flew overhead, we covered our ears and had to get out and hide in the ditches, crawling out only when night came and we could travel under cover of darkness. The villagers didn't even get off the road and went on as if nothing unusual were happening. Farther down the road we had to drive around the skeletons of tanks and other vehicles that were still on fire in the middle of the road. Even now, almost a day later, I can still smell the sharp odor of explosions and burning tires.

The villages we pass are a blur of dust, barefoot children, and women in burkas. The little girls wear clothes once brightly colored but now old and faded. In every village it seems a funeral is going on. At one place we see a wedding. There are musicians playing the *saz* and drums and women dancing with their best clothes on. A few miles past the village I see through the dust-covered window of the bus a white horse galloping riderless down the valley.

As we approach Kandahar over the winding mountain roads, I begin to feel a different kind of tension and anxiety, knowing that we will soon be there.

I open my eyes with a jerk and see the trees alongside the bus running away from me. My mouth is dry and there is a throbbing against my temples. My back hurts and I know that the bus ride hasn't been good for my kidneys. Zamirvali puts his hand on my shoulder.

"Are you okay?" he asks. "You were talking in your sleep."

He pours a cup of water and hands it to me. The warm water soothes my mouth and throat as it goes down. Cup in hand, I watch the water jump out with each bump and jerk of the bus and struggle to keep it from spilling as my dream plays out before my eyes.

. . . I'm in the house in Shiraz, lying in bed beside Shireen. She has her red dress on and is turned toward the door. Her black hair is pushed to one side and her long lashes are interlocked. She looks sad, sadder than I've ever seen her. I caress her back slowly up and down. I sense a slight change of light in the room, and when I turn and look toward the door, I see a shadow there. My hand stops on the curve of her back and at that moment the shadow disappears. I think I saw Ruzbeh standing there. I get up and go through the dark hallway and down the stairs. The creaking steps are shaking. It must be an earthquake. Everything is shaking. The whole house is shaking and the walls are splitting. I try to hold onto the railings, but they break off in my hands and the steps give way under my feet.

Twenty-five

I CAN HARDLY KEEP my eyes open and have no idea where we are when Zamirvali tells me in a tired voice that we have arrived, that we are in the outskirts of Kandahar. All through the trip I have been thinking about Shireen traveling the same roads, wondering whether she had been in this place or that and how she felt when the bus went through the checkpoints. Now that I'm here, I can't imagine what her condition or frame of mind will be.

It's early afternoon, and the sun is hot. The bus passes through a gate into a large, open garage. Parked on one side are several buses and minibuses and an old, brightly painted truck. People rush around noisily with their bundles, the men carrying them on their backs, the women on their heads. I've never seen so many women totally covered with burkas. Even their faces are hidden behind the woven screen in front of their eyes. I watch cautiously, wondering what dark-eyed beauty might be hidden under the somber coverings.

After walking up and down to get the blood circulating in my legs, I go to a water tap by the gate to wash. The porters are pushing carts around. A donkey attached to a cart is standing still, its head bowed and its tail snapping constantly to drive away the many flies. The place is dusty, and there is a sharp smell of onions, garlic, turmeric, and cooking oil. I feel exhausted and my body aches. We have to wait until the load is down from the top of the bus and Zamirvali has picked up his bundle and his suitcase. I have only the shoulder bag with all my belongings, that I've been carrying throughout the trip.

Zamirvali talks to the taxi drivers and bargains for the fare. Finally, he settles with one of them and we get into a rickety old taxi. We go through a few streets and around a rotary. In the center a group of red banners with hammers and sickles flap in the air. As we speed through the narrow alleys, I think that a door is going to fly open or fall off any moment. With every bump my head hits the roof. Finally we stop in front of an iron gate with peeling blue paint. Zamirvali helps me out of the taxi. A few women covered in burkas walk by.

Two girls who are six or seven and a small boy come to the gate and run to Zamirvali. He bends down and kisses them, then picks up the boy and holds him up in the air, looking at him with a bright smile. "*Pesaram, bozorg shodi baba-jan*—You've grown bigger, my son," he says joyfully.

He pushes the door open and invites me to go in ahead of him. "*Befarma'id*—please come in. We're home."

The small courtyard is surrounded by a low brick wall. Could it be that Shireen is here? I look around but don't see any sign of her. There are two rooms on one side of the yard with doors that are also painted a faded blue. A clothesline running across the yard is hung with children's clothes. A child's bicycle with one wheel missing is propped in a corner. In a bare area at the end of the small garden, a white goat is tied to a weeping-willow tree. The ends of the low branches are missing as far up as the goat can reach.

"Is Shireen here?" I ask Zamirvali.

"Yes. Welcome to our home."

I take off my turban and stand against the wall, not wanting to move. I look toward the two doors. It seems impossible to believe she is behind one of them. There is only a door between us, just a door, like that last night in Shiraz.

The anxiety is killing me, and I almost call out. Then one of the doors opens and a woman in a brown burka steps out. My heartbeat quickens and I move toward her. Then, hearing an Afghan accent, I stop.

"*Salaam. Khush amadid be manzel ma*—Hello, you're welcome in our house."

Zamirvali turns to her. "Where is Shireen Khanom?"

"She's gone to the school to see the teacher," the woman says.

"Go get her," he says. "Just tell her I've come from Shiraz."

I watch as she runs into the alley.

"School?" I ask Zamirvali.

"Yes, we have a little school in this neighborhood. It's close by. That was my wife. She'll bring her. Please, let's go inside."

The children hang on to Zamirvali's baggy pants. I don't want to move and stand there against the wall, weak and dizzy. I close my eyes for a while and then open them as the children laugh and run around the yard, wearing their gifts of bright-yellow plastic sunglasses.

The courtyard gate opens, and a woman walks in with Zamirvali's wife. I look closer. She is wearing a long green Afghani dress and a yellow scarf. She nods at Zamirvali and then looks at me.

"Behruz?" she says, staring in disbelief.

Am I imagining that I'm hearing her voice? It can't be, I think. I haven't heard her voice since we were children.

"Behruz?" I hear her again. "Is it you? My God! How did you get here?"

I rush to her.

She opens her arms. I hold her, feeling her warmth and smelling the sweet scent of her hair. Feeling me trembling, she holds me tighter.

It's as if I've always heard her voice, always heard her talking to me.

I look at her and then hug her again. "Oh, dear Shireen. Shireen-*aziz*. I can't believe you're alive and in my arms." I'm overwhelmed and can't keep back my tears.

"And you—I can't believe you're here in front me." She kisses me on both cheeks. Then she steps back and with a smile looks at me as if she wants to take in the sight of me in my Afghani clothes.

"It's like a dream, an impossibility, I'm so happy to see you." She wipes her eyes with the end of her scarf.

I can't understand how it is possible that she is talking after so many years. Did Farideh know—why didn't she tell me? Maybe she knew I wouldn't believe it unless I heard her myself.

"Shireen—your voice . . . ?"

"Yes. It came back," she says. "I can't explain it."

I look at her through my tears and remember the spring day in the Naranjestan when we were children playing at having a wedding . . . Could it be that first awful event shocked her so that she became mute while the later one had the opposite effect? I look at her in silence. She looks very thin and there is a darkness around her green eyes, but they have the same familiar sparks. When I look more closely, I can see a few faint scars on her forehead and chin.

She smiles, looking at me as if to convince herself I'm really here. All at once I feel overcome and break into tears, hiding my face in my hands.

"I'm sorry," I say after a minute. "I'm sorry I ran away, I'm sorry for all the pain I caused you and Ruzbeh." I speak in a low voice. I'm exhausted and light-headed.

"Here is my room," she says, taking my arm. "Let's go in."

I realize that Zamirvali and his wife and children, their plastic glasses still on, are standing there watching us. We go into her small room. A chill runs through me and I know my fever is returning. I tell myself that I have to fight it, that now is the time to be strong.

"Are you okay?" Shireen asks in a worried voice. "You look ill. Why don't you lie down?"

"Yes," I say calmly, not wanting to worry her, "I'm just tired. It's the stress of being on the road. I'll be fine." But I wonder if I really will be fine, the way my bladder and kidneys feel.

Zamirvali brings a blanket, and Shireen covers me with it.

"You don't look okay to me," she says. "You may be sick. You can get sick very easily in this country. I'll get you some water."

The room has one small window and the walls are bare except for the mirror hanging next to the door. She comes back with a glass of water and hands it to me. "You need to rest. I have so many questions to ask you, but I can wait. Just tell me any news you have from Ruzbeh."

"He's safe," I say.

"Where is he? Is he all right?"

"He's fine. He's back in Shiraz."

"Shiraz?"

"Yes. He is staying with Farideh and Javid."

"Oh, thank God. And my mother, and your mother?"

"They're still in the village."

"After I came here," she says, "you can't believe how things started to come back to me. Everything was blank for months—Ruzbeh, you, our mothers. Everything that happened. Until I came here. Even most of the trip to Kandahar was a blur. I had a high fever and wasn't myself during the cold nights on the road.

"The amazing thing," she continues near tears, "is that on the bus coming here, Zamirvali poured a cup of tea for me and when he handed it to me, I said, 'thank you,' and at that moment I thought I heard myself, that it wasn't just in my head. I said, 'thank you, Zamirvali, you're very kind.' He smiled and I knew he had heard me. I sat quiet. I wasn't excited. I was sad in a way at that moment, I don't know exactly why. I stared out through the bus window, holding the tea. How was it possible? Then I remembered . . . I remembered how at that terrible moment in the square I had screamed as loud as I could . . ."

She becomes quiet, looking at me and smiling. I can see she is thinking. "After a couple of weeks of rest here," she says, "things started to come back to me in fragments. I thought about all of you day and night and didn't know what to do except try to be strong, gather up the pieces, and go on."

I listen to her soft voice and feel like I don't want to think about anything, past or present. I just want to be in the moment, sit and listen to her, comfort her if I can.

"I need to ask you about so many things," she says, "but not now. You need to rest." She wipes her eyes. "Just tell me one more thing. What happened to you?" She stares at me. "You are so thin. Are you ill?"

I wonder how I can talk about what has happened to me after what she has gone through.

"I'm fine," I say. "I found Ruzbeh and I found you. That's what I wanted more than anything. I want Ruzbeh to come here. I want to make things right again."

Zamirvali brings a pot of tea and fills the glass cups. He puts a cup in front of me and one in front of Shireen and then puts a bowl of sugar cubes between us. His wife comes in with a big dish of oranges and pomegranates and leaves quietly.

A scratching feeling starts in the back of my throat and makes me cough, a hard cough that I can't control and brings tears to my eyes. This is something new, I think. Shireen holds me until I can stop shaking.

"You must rest," she says. "You need a doctor. I'll go get a doctor—I know one."

I don't want her to leave. I don't want her out of my sight and am afraid she will disappear again.

"Stay for now. Stay," I say. "I'm okay. Let's just have some tea and oranges."

She picks up an orange, holding it in her palm momentarily before starting to peel it. My God, she is so beautiful, I say to myself. I don't want to take my eyes off her, but as she goes on talking in her soft voice I find my eyes closing.

Twenty-six

I N T H E D A Y S T H A T Zamirvali was getting ready to return to
Shiraz, I asked him if he could take back two letters we had for
Javid and Ruzbeh. To my surprise, he said he couldn't. "It would be
dangerous because at the border and at the checkpoints they look at
everything, searching for drugs entering Iran, and also if they find
any evidence of human trafficking, I'll end up in jail."

"On my last trip," he said, "I had a letter from Shireen Khanom.
I was frightened. They saw it and I was lucky they didn't open it.
I would do anything for Mr. Javid Rahimi, but I have a wife and
children. I need to be careful. If they find out I brought you here
illegally, I could be arrested by our communists here or the Iranians
on the other side of the border."

Both Shireen and I were disappointed, but there was nothing we
could do and we knew it would be too risky to send the letters by
mail, especially since Javid had warned us against it. The day before
the trip, though, Shireen was at school and Zamirvali came to the
room and indicated he was willing to take the letters.

"Are you sure?" I asked surprised.

"Inshallah there'll be no problem. I've figured out a way to take them."

He handed me a light-yellow shawl that he had bought in the bazaar and asked me to write the letters in a long line and as small as I could along the edges. His plan was to roll the shawl as a turban and wear it at the border crossing.

I got to work right away, spreading out the cloth on a tray and using a blue ballpoint pen to write my letter as discreetly as I could alongside one edge, leaving the other edge for Shireen.

Dear ones,

I'm here with S in the outskirts of Kandahar. I arrived last week and found her in high spirits, her eyes shining as I remember. You can't imagine how wonderful it was for me to find her. It was as if after wandering in the desert for days I had found a tree to rest under. Her strength and spirit are immeasurable.

Thanks to both of you, I made it here, although I was ill all through the trip and still am. But I won't bother you with that now. Our friend is a brave and honest man and brought me safely here. Without him it would have been impossible. His family, with all the limitations they face, have done the best they could for S.

I hope my brother is still with you and his health is better. Please go ahead with what we talked about. Please do this as quickly as you can. I haven't been well enough since I got here to see about going to our destination, but S has contacted the people whose names you gave her. It's going to take a while—they won't tell us exactly—for things to be arranged. We'll be ready by the time R gets here and hope we can make it to a U.N. or Red Cross refugee office. S says there is a telephone and telegraph office in the center of the town. We'll call you in a week if the lines are working—I know it could be risky—just to find out if you got the letters and when R will be on the way.

I will stop here. Please let our friends at the village know I'm well. I owe my life to all of you. Thank you again.

With love and friendship,

B

My dearest one,

What can I say and where can I start? Oh, some things are not meant to be written down. How I wish you were here and I could tell you everything. You know how much I love you and my love is as strong as ever. That's how I survived the unimaginable—love pulled me through, and now I want you to be with me. I don't know how much you know and don't know. I can't deny what happened. I certainly can't deny what happened to me, or to you or to your brother.

Oh, my dear, your brother is ill. He doesn't admit it but I think it is something serious and am not sure he will survive it—something with his kidneys. I don't know what he has gone through over these past months. He doesn't tell me. I'm sorry to send you this news. The doctor here is not very optimistic and I don't have the heart to tell B that. The doctor advises that he be hospitalized. Medical facilities are very limited here. I asked the doctor not to say anything to him, but I'm sure he knows it himself. I'm writing because I want you to come so we can go to Canada or America, both of you can receive proper medical care, and hopefully we can start a new life.

I don't want to tell you in a letter what I have gone through or what happened when you kept running away from me. I know you were thinking of me and that as soon as the signs were there you went away. Those two years were the hardest time for me. Did we make mistakes? I don't think so, because it was our love that was the source of the strength and hope that kept us alive and helped us through each day. I'm sorry I left without seeing you. I didn't know where you were.

You must come. And please, before you come, go to my mother. And your mother. Tell them that I'm alive and that I'm safe where I am. I wasn't able to go to the village because I didn't want them to see me in the condition I was in. Judging from what B tells me, it is possible that they may have some idea of what happened. I'm waiting for you and will have things arranged by the time you get here. Do you remember how we wanted to go to America? How we wanted to meet B's friend? It might be possible now. B is sending her a letter. She teaches at a school in South Dakota. I hope they can be back together. The way he talks about her, it's obvious he still loves her. When we're there, we'll learn English. And we can have another chance at life.

Oh, before I forget, please bring warm clothes. It's cold here and they say it will be much colder by next month. And be careful on the road. Make sure to take your medicine and make sure to bring enough with you for the trip and the time to follow.

I want to tell you what makes me go on these days in this beautiful and at the same time awful place—beautiful because of the wonderful people who have nothing to offer except kindness and awful because of the ongoing war and destruction. I have been able to go on because I'm doing something that makes me hopeful. In a two-room school I'm teaching small children who have lost their hearing from explosions. I'm teaching them to communicate by sign language and they love it. We also have a tiny garden in the school yard. We've planted geraniums and roses. They know all about you and the Naranjestan. They draw flowers and gardens and rainbows. I'm sending one of the drawings—it's a picture of you and me walking under the lemon trees of the Naranjestan. I had told them about our orchard of sweet lemons.

Come and bring a dozen colored pencils for us. I love you with my all heart.

S

Twenty-seven

S HIREEN COMES IN, her gaze vibrant. "I'm so happy," she says. "I feel I could fly."

She's wearing the earrings that were Ruzbeh's gift. They are long and the green of the turquoise complements her eyes.

"Well, well," I say with a smile. "You must have finally succeeded in talking to Ruzbeh."

"Yes," she says and hands me a candy. "I bought these for my schoolchildren. You can have one."

"And?" I ask anxiously.

"He's coming. He'll be on the road in three days. He said it was very good that we sent those letters. And—and I also went to see Noorahmad, the man who is going to take us to Pakistan. He said everything is arranged and we should be ready to leave in two weeks. He said there will be snow soon, and the roads will become dangerous."

She makes sure the blanket is covering me. "It is true," she says. "It's getting colder every day."

"And I'm burning up from fever in here. Noorahmad didn't ask for more money, did he?"

"No."

"Good. What else did Ruzbeh say?"

"Well, he couldn't believe it was me talking, but then . . ." She hesitates.

"What?"

"He said he felt that half of him wasn't there." She gives me another candy. "Did you take your medicine?"

"Yes, I did. What else did he say?"

"He sounded fine—you know, like when he was well. He said that the Indian doctor—Dr. Sharma—has been very helpful. He's giving him something that helps him with his headaches so he can sleep and rest. Farideh has been very good in helping him also. He said he misses us and has decided to come. He wanted to talk to you, thinking you were with me. I didn't tell him you aren't feeling well. The connection wasn't good at all. I got disconnected twice, and the young man there—Mostefa, you remember him? He was in the office when we went there last week?—he dialed and dialed, but he couldn't get through. I asked him to try again." She laughs. "You know me. I wouldn't give up that easily. Finally he connected the call again. I guess it was our lucky day. But I couldn't say much on the phone. I didn't mention Afghanistan, Kandahar, or Pakistan. I didn't want to risk anything. Anyway, Ruzbeh said to tell you that he has something in the palm of his hand, something from long ago—he said you would understand."

It takes a minute for my mind to travel back to our childhood days. I nod and smile.

She looks at me and then goes on. "I also talked to Farideh briefly. We were excited hearing each other's voices. She said they were planning a trip to the north—not immediately, but soon. Maybe she was trying to tell me something. Didn't you say they were planning to leave the country too?"

She grows quiet for a moment and looks out into the yard. There is something different about her. Something in her eyes, or in her face—I can't tell what—as if she is thinking of the past, or is it the future?

"Wouldn't it be wonderful if we all could be together again?" she says.

"Of course," I answer, wondering about such a possibility.

She stays quiet for a long time, looking at me lying under the blanket, my forehead damp with perspiration.

"Behruz?" she says and waits. "Do you think he's coming? Or is he just saying that?"

"He's coming," I say.

"How can you be sure?"

"From something you said."

"What?"

I wait.

"What? Tell me."

"Do you remember our summers in the Naranjestan? When we were little, I mean. Ruzbeh had a game."

"What game?" she breaks in.

"One you didn't know about. Summer nights we would go up to the roof of the farmhouse and look at the stars. We would hold our arms up high and try to catch a star. Sometimes we thought of the stars as girls."

She laughs, her eyes lighting up.

"We would close our palms and bring them down to see if we had caught one. I never did, but Ruzbeh always said he did. He would open his palm, saying, 'Here, here! I got one!' 'Who?' I would ask. 'Shireen,' he would say. Every time it would be you."

She blushes.

"It's true, and we believed it. We did. When he opened his palm, I would see a soft floating light there."

She stays quiet for a while. "I miss him, Behruz," she says finally. "I miss him so much. I miss it all—our mothers, our home, the lemon grove."

She wipes away her tears. "Behruz, tell me . . ."

"Tell you what?"

"It won't be like home where we are going, will it? . . ."

I hesitate, looking at her moist eyes.

"Even if it isn't," she says, "we have to go. We have to go on."

I stay quiet since she has answered her own question.